Suddenly Data heard a shuffling sound ahead of him.

One of the cadets must have slipped. They all froze in terror as Pen Sziid's tinny voice snapped, "There was a noise."

"Lukas, T'Pira, run!" Fantico whispered urgently. "We'll cover you!" Lukas and T'Pira dashed away as Fantico ordered, "Data, Zhu, show them you're unarmed."

Obediently, Data held out his empty hands and turned to face the Dyrondites, who rounded the far corner of the passageway and stared at the cadets with bland expressions. Apparently, Pon Shaab didn't notice that Data was unarmed, or he didn't care. He calmly raised a disruptor. "Data, look out!" Fantico yelled.

But there was nowhere to go. A blast of light filled the passageway and Data felt a hot bolt of energy strike the middle of his chest. His limbs froze and he slammed to the ground, a high-pitched electronic squeal ripping through his circuits.

Then everything went black.

Star Trek: The Next Generation
STARFLEET ACADEMY

#1 Worf's First Adventure
#2 Line of Fire
#3 Survival
#4 Capture the Flag
#5 Atlantis Station
#6 Mystery of the Missing Crew
#7 Secret of the Lizard People
#8 Starfall
#9 Nova Command
#10 Loyalties
#11 Crossfire
#12 Breakaway
#13 The Haunted Starship
#14 Deceptions

Star Trek:
STARFLEET ACADEMY

#1 Crisis on Vulcan
#2 Aftershock
#3 Cadet Kirk

Star Trek: Deep Space Nine

#1 The Star Ghost
#2 Stowaways
#3 Prisoners of Peace
#4 The Pet
#5 Arcade
#6 Field Trip
#7 Gypsy World
#8 Highest Score
#9 Cardassian Imps
#10 Space Camp
#11 Day of Honor: Honor
    Bound
#12 Trapped in Time

Star Trek: Voyager
STARFLEET ACADEMY

#1 Lifeline
#2 The Chance Factor
#3 Quarantine

Star Trek movie tie-ins

Star Trek Generations
Star Trek First Contact

Available from MINSTREL Books

STAR TREK
THE NEXT GENERATION®

STARFLEET ACADEMY® #14

DECEPTIONS

Bobbi JG Weiss & David Cody Weiss

Interior illustrations by
Jason Palmer

A MINSTREL® BOOK

Published by POCKET BOOKS
New York   London   Toronto   Sydney   Tokyo   Singapore

A MINSTREL PAPERBACK *Original*

A Minstrel Book published by
POCKET BOOKS, a division of Simon & Schuster Inc.
1230 Avenue of the Americas, New York, NY 10020

This book is published by Pocket Books, a division of Simon & Schuster Inc., under exclusive license from Paramount Pictures.

ISBN: 0-671-01723-3

First Minstrel Books printing April 1998

10 9 8 7 6 5 4 3 2 1

A MINSTREL BOOK and colophon are registered trademarks of Simon & Schuster Inc.

Cover art by Donato Giancola

Printed in the U.S.A.

*To Michael, who's got the logic,
to Jay, who's got the ears,
and to Shane, who's got it all.*

CHRONOLOGY

2167

Iwasaki "Ike" Ikushima graduates from Starfleet Academy.

2179

Benjamin Franklin launched with Ikushima in command. Billy Devil killed in the Battle of the Belt.

2181

Ikushima dies following shipboard accident.

2332

Bernardo O'H. Sanchez born.

2335

Geordi La Forge born.

2336

Sanchez's father leaves Spacedock aboard Enterprise-C.

2344

Enterprise-C lost in defense of Narendra III.

2350

Sanchez enters Starfleet Academy.

2353

La Forge enters Starfleet Academy.

2354

<u>Benjamin Franklin</u> leaves Spacedock on routine training mission.

CHAPTER

1

The room was dark except for a single circle of illumination on one wall. Within that circle, the shadow of a dog's head took form. The dog's mouth opened and closed, opened and closed, in a silent barking spree. It wiggled one ear, bobbed up and down a few times, and then its tongue flopped out of its mouth as it started to pant.

At least, that was what Data tried to make it do. The problem was that his fingers were already so twisted up he couldn't quite find a free finger to make a tongue.

"Data, I be in your presence," came a voice through the darkness.

Data already knew that the voice belonged to his roommate, Zhu Lniuhta'bihd, and he turned his head to see the small Tangonese cadet standing in the doorway.

Data had said time and again that his android ears could hear Zhu's approach from halfway down the hall, and he could even recognize the pattern of Zhu's footsteps, as there was a slight shuffle to his walk because of the higher gravity on Earth compared to that on Tangoni IX. But Tangonese courtesy required Zhu to alert anyone alone in a room to his presence, even when entering his own dorm room.

Zhu stared at Data's contorted fingers, held up against the light. "What be you doing?" he asked curiously.

"I am attempting to form a shadow canine," Data explained, and to illustrate, he made his dog bark again. "However, I seem to be in need of more fingers."

Zhu chuckled. "You be very odd. Everyone else in the dorm be breaking their skulls studying, and here be you playing with your fingers."

Data lowered his hands. "On the contrary, my present activity is part of my extracurricular studies. At various times in Earth history, the manipulation of shadow images has been considered an art form."

"As I understand, so be spitting," Zhu countered.

"Really?" Data quickly searched his memory banks. No records related spitting with art forms, however. The android shot Zhu a quizzical stare. "Are you certain?"

The Tangonese chuckled again. "Data, you be very entertaining. I be glad you be my roommate." Data wasn't sure exactly what that was supposed to mean, but before he could ask, Zhu continued, "I be here to ask a favor. I must take an astrophysics exam tomorrow, and I be wondering if you have time to help me."

"Help you what?"

Again Zhu chuckled. Data noted how often Zhu

chuckled in his presence and wondered if the Tangonese chuckled as much in the presence of other cadets. "Help me study. What else?"

"Oh. Certainly." Data tilted his head up. "Computer, normal illumination, please." The lights gradually came up. Data switched off his desk lamp. "What aspect of astrophysics do you wish to review?"

"Actually," Zhu replied, taking a firm hold of Data's arm, "my notes be in the study lounge. May we go there?"

Data barely managed to say, "Of course," before Zhu pulled him out into the hallway.

By now the android was used to helping his dorm-mates study. At least once a day somebody came to him with a class-related question. "What year was the Treaty of Algeron made?" "What is the atomic weight of eitanium?" "How can I solve Fermat's last theorem?" Since Data usually had time to spare, he was more than willing to help. He thought it only fair, since many subjects that cadets found difficult were easy for him, such as math, engineering, history, and hard sciences.

On the other hand, in the three months since his arrival at Starfleet Academy, Data had noticed that the subjects most cadets found easiest were the hardest for him. Philosophy, cultural studies, and interspecies diplomacy, for instance, often baffled him. Data possessed no emotions, and he struggled with abstract concepts like art, belief systems, or even fashion. He hoped that, in time, he would experience enough in his own life to finally understand the behavior of living beings, humans especially.

Data and Zhu reached the study lounge on the opposite end of the dorm building. Zhu stepped forward to activate the automatic door. When it *whooshed* open, he politely gestured Data inside. "After you."

"Thank you." Data stepped through to find the lounge filled with the usual assortment of cadets seated at tables, slouched on couches, or even sprawled on the floor, every one of them engrossed in study. But suddenly they all whirled to face him.

"Surprise!" Party hats appeared from under desks and behind stacks of data padds. Several cadets threw confetti in the air, and Cadet Cynthia Gallingston dashed over to Data and plopped a bright red party hat with a goofy green tassel on his head.

"Happy birthday!" she said, and kissed him on the cheek.

Data was unable to react in surprise the way a human could, but his programming compelled him to take a step back, his eyes widening. "You are mistaken, Cynthia," he said. "I am an android. I do not have a birthday."

"Oh yes you do!" said Zhu, accepting a blazing purple party hat from Cynthia. He put it on his head, carefully pushing it back so that it wouldn't cover the intricate tattoo on his forehead. The tattoo signified Zhu's clan and family, and to cover it was taboo among his people. "The day you be discovered on Omicron Theta be, in a sense, your birthday," Zhu continued. "I looked up your records and found the date—exactly three years ago today."

Data regarded his roommate closely. "You said we were to study for your astrophysics test tomorrow."

"Oh, that be just to get you in here," laughed Zhu.

"So you do *not* have an astrophysics test tomorrow?"

"No, I *do* have an astrophysics test tomorrow," Zhu patiently explained, "but I know the material. I just told you I needed your help in order to bring you here without spoiling the surprise."

"Then you purposely gave me inaccurate information." Data paused, disturbed. "You lied to me."

"No, I didn't."

Data opened his mouth to protest, but Zhu held up his hands in surrender.

"Okay, I did. Data, a surprise birthday party be pointless unless it be a surprise. This be a case where deception be not wrong. It be like a game." When Data only looked more disturbed, Zhu added, "You often speak of wanting to understand humans. Here be your chance. I researched Earth and discovered that birthdays be celebrated throughout history by almost every society here. Don't you want to experience what it be all about?"

Data slowly nodded as his ethics program struggled to justify deceit as a means to a positive end. Unaware of the android's internal dilemma, Zhu and Cynthia guided him to a table where somebody had placed a birthday cake with white frosting and blue trim. Little sugar decorations shaped like machine parts were artistically placed around a line of red frosting that spelled out Happy Birthday Data! Three candles burned brightly in the center of the cake.

"Okay, make a wish and blow out the candles," Cynthia instructed.

Data looked at her. "Why?"

A handsome, dark-skinned human, Waylyn Marks, sighed loudly. "Because that's what a birthday boy does. You wish for something, blow out the candles, and if

7

you blow the candles out in only one breath, your wish will come true."

Data cocked his head. "What relationship does the termination of a flame have with wish fulfillment?"

Everybody groaned. "Just do it!" Zhu begged, and the others hooted agreement.

Data wondered what to wish for. He could wish to be human, but of course, that was impossible. He could wish to know who made him and why, but he was somehow sure that the mystery of his origin couldn't be solved by simple wishing. He finally decided to wish for a successful Starfleet career. After all, he intended to spend a good deal of his life in Starfleet, however long his life might last. He blew the candles out in one breath and everybody clapped. Five minutes later, nothing was left of the cake but crumbs.

Afterwards, the cadets showered Data with presents. Most of them were silly things, like a squeaking rubber ducky or a gag commbadge that squirted water. Data was fascinated by each item, even though he didn't understand most of them. He intended to ask Zhu about them later.

Zhu waited to present his gift just as the party came to an end. "Here," he said, and handed Data a small package.

Data carefully opened the wrapping paper and found a memory chip inside a little box. The surface of the chip was inscribed with a miniature version of the tattoo on Zhu's forehead. "In my culture, an inscribed blank book be given to a family member on their Day of Maturity. The book be for their first journal entries."

"But I do not keep a journal," Data informed him.

"There is no need. My internal memory automatically records every event that I experience in complete detail."

"I know that," Zhu said, "but on my world, a journal be not used to record events, but one's thoughts and reflections *about* those events."

"Ah." Data paused, looking down at the chip in his hand. "But I do not need a storage chip to do that either, Zhu. My internal memory can hold—"

"The chip be a symbolic gift, Data."

"Ah," Data said again. He finally understood that Zhu's gift was actually the suggestion to start a journal. That intrigued the android. He'd often watched Zhu compose his own journal entries, wondering what the Tangonese was writing about. Tangonese tradition required that each mature person keep a journal of their thoughts about the events in their lives, so that each person's life experience could be preserved forever.

"Celebrating the life of a living person is silly," Zhu had once explained to the android. "We Tangonese celebrate the death dates of our ancestors, for only after death can the worth of a life be truly assessed. The degree of celebration for each person be evaluated after death according to family's and friends' memories, and the journal." Data recalled how Zhu had added proudly, "I hope to live a great and honorable life so that I be celebrated with joy after I be gone."

Carefully replacing the box's lid, Data said, "This is a most thoughtful gift, Zhu. Yes, I think I would like to start a journal."

Zhu beamed with pleasure. "Perhaps analyzing your

interactions with others be helpful to you in understanding humans and emotions."

That night, Data sat at his desk, thinking about all the strange events of the day. Then he created a new file in his internal memory system, labeled it Journal, and began to compose.

This will be my first journal entry. I understand that most humans who keep such records begin each entry with a greeting to the journal itself. Although I do not understand why an inanimate object should be addressed thus, I shall follow convention.

Dear Diary,
My fellow cadets organized a surprise birthday celebration for me today. I still debate whether I actually have a birthday, but the experience was strangely gratifying. Most fascinating was the fact that my roommate, Zhu Lniuhta'bihd, employed deception to create the element of surprise. No one at the party objected to such questionable behavior, and in fact, they all seemed quite pleased that the deception succeeded. I will have to study this further.

Sincerely,
Data

CHAPTER

2

Of all the classes he was taking that semester, Data preferred xenoethnography the most. A branch of anthropology, it dealt with the scientific description of alien cultures. It never ceased to amaze the android how many life-forms existed in the galaxy, how different they all were, and yet how surprisingly similar they were.

Xenoethnography was his first class the morning after his birthday party. Just before the class ended, Data's instructor, Aika Watanabe, made an announcement. "Cadets, next week we will not meet for regular instruction," she said. "This class and the other two xenoethnography classes will embark on a three-day field trip off-planet. You'll be divided into groups. Each group will travel to a different planet or starbase to participate in various archaeological digs and observe how archaeologists run their operations. Such operations are an example of one of the Federation's basic functions, the exploration of new civilizations, whether those civilizations are modern or ancient ones.

"Each group will be assigned a junior-year command-track cadet as leader. Your leaders will be contacting you within the next twenty-four hours to set up a briefing, during which time your group's assignment will be described in detail and any questions you have will be answered. When you return from your trips, each group will be expected to present a detailed report to the class."

Data found himself looking forward to the trip. The last time he'd been off Earth was to observe a super-Jovian planet ignition, an event that had become more of an adventure than he'd expected. What might he encounter at an archaeological dig on a far-off planet?

That evening when he returned to his dorm room after classes, he found a message waiting on his comm padd. "Cadet Data, this is Ejay Fantico, your team leader for the xenoethnography field trip. I will be holding a briefing tomorrow evening at nineteen hundred hours in the Excelsior Room of Cochrane Hall. Please be prompt."

Data turned to Zhu, who was lying on his bed, absorbed in a text on navigation theory. "Have you received a communication from your team leader?" he asked. Zhu was also taking xenoethnography that semester, though he was in a different class than Data.

"Yes," Zhu said flatly. "It also be from Cadet Fantico."

Data brightened. "Then we are on the same team."

Zhu said nothing. He didn't even raise his eyes from his text.

Data waited, but clearly Zhu wasn't going to speak further. "Is something wrong?" he finally asked with concern.

"Yes. I be not wanting to go to an archaeological dig."

"Why?"

Zhu hesitated. "I be afraid."

That was the last thing Data expected to hear. Then again, his roommate's fear might stem from the fact that the Tangonese people, though friendly, were known to be shy around strangers. Zhu had been terrified of Data when they'd first met. Then, after they'd gotten to know each other, Zhu had come to depend heavily on Data in most social situations. Data had found it gratifying to be needed in such a way, just as he'd found it gratifying to drill Zhu in Standard Federation English. The complex Tangonese language had only one form of the verb to be, so although Zhu had mastered most other English verb forms, he still couldn't quite master "to be." However, with Data's help, he was learning to interact with other cadets more easily.

With a troubled sigh, Zhu set his navigation text aside. "The remains of the dead should be not disturbed," he said. "It be wrong."

"Why?"

"You have no ancestors, Data. You be not able to understand. But I be afraid to go."

"You must go," Data said. "It is a class requirement."

Zhu frowned. "Yes, I must go. But I be reluctant to do so."

*   *   *

At 1900 hours the next evening, Data and Zhu entered the Excelsior Room of Cochrane Hall to find two other freshman cadets already seated at the only table there. One of them, a Vulcan female with piercing blue eyes, said, "Greetings. I am T'Pira. This is Lukas Whitlock."

Lukas, a tall, lanky human with a wide smile, leaned back in his chair and lazily waved his hand. "Howdy."

"Howdy to you also," Data answered, hoping he'd responded correctly. He'd never heard the word howdy before, but it sounded like a greeting. "I am Data, and this is Zhu Lniuhta'bihd."

With sudden energy, Lukas leaned forward. "You're Data? The android? Wow!" He jumped up from his chair. "Can I take a look at you?" Before Data could answer, he leaned close up to Data's face as if he wanted

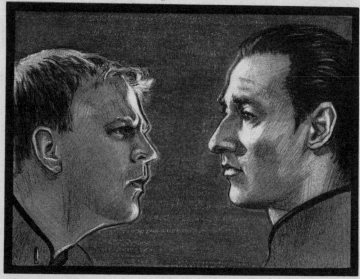

to bite his nose. "You're a doggone miracle," he murmured, gawking into Data's yellow eyes.

Data stared back. "What do miracles have to do with absent canines?"

"Huh?" said Lukas. Then he grinned. "Absent canines—doggone." He laughed. "You've even got a sense of humor!"

"That is incorrect," Data said. "I have no sense of humor. I have no emotions at all."

"Oh." Lukas scratched his chin. "Too bad. Funny comeback, though."

T'Pira tapped Lukas's arm. Such familiarity suggested to Data that she and Lukas were already friends. "Lukas, would it not be wise to resume your seat? Cadet Fantico will be here at any moment."

"Cadet Fantico *is* here." A young woman strode into the room, short, compact, and pretty, despite the fact that she pursed her lips so hard they turned white. "Let's bring this meeting to order."

As Data lowered himself into a chair, Lukas whispered in his ear, "She's nervous." Data made no reply. For one thing, he couldn't tell if Fantico was nervous or not, and second, he knew better than to make personal comments about superiors, especially in their presence.

"Good evening, cadets," Fantico began, setting four data padds on the table. "Let me start off by saying that this trip is designed to be a test for all of us. I need your cooperation to succeed as much as you need mine. If we all do our jobs, I think we can make our instructors, and ourselves, proud."

Data saw that Fantico was following the first rule of leadership: create a sense of good-fellowship within the group. He, of course, had no intention of doing anything but his best on this assignment, but he understood that biological beings often required encouragement in order to perform at their best.

"Our destination is the planet Arunu," Fantico told the group, "the third planet in the Karei System. An archaeological team headed by Professor Jeffrey Spinaker has been there for several months now studying recently discovered ruins of the Arunuan civilization. Have any of you heard of the Arunuans?"

Data held up his hand. "The Arunuan people are presumed to have existed some four hundred thousand years ago. Ancient texts from the Oolimfu and Boodinji peoples of the third planet of the Karei System speak of a visiting group of 'silent ones,' suggesting that the Arunuans did not speak aloud. Little else is known of them, except that they must have possessed the capacity for limited space travel to have made an appearance on their sister planet."

Fantico stared at him. "Um, that is correct, Mr. Data."

T'Pira caught the android's eye, her expression hinting at admiration. Lukas gave Data a thumbs up.

"Arunu itself," Ejay finally continued, "is a dead world—no animal or plant life. There is little water, and none of it is drinkable. The archaeological team comprises the only life on the entire surface. You will all be required to wear oxygenation masks while there. The air is breathable, but its oxygen content is far too low to support human life for more than a minute or two." Fantico turned to Data. "Even though you don't need to breathe like biological life-forms, Mr. Data, you will

be required to wear a mask as well, as per standard Starfleet regulations for cadets."

"Of course, sir," Data responded, "though I must correct your information. Although I do not need to breathe for survival purposes, a periodic intake of air is necessary to cool my internal systems."

This time Fantico smiled. "I stand corrected, Mr. Data. You're quite a fount of explanations, aren't you?"

"I endeavor to be, sir," Data declared.

Fantico continued. "Okay, each of you is responsible for arranging leave from your other classes. This field trip is an established freshman venture, so your other instructors shouldn't give you any trouble. However, you will be responsible for keeping up with your other classwork while away. Each night you will receive your homework assignments by subspace communiqué, and each morning you must relay your finished assignments back. Understood?"

Data and his peers nodded.

"Well, then, take these data padds with you," and she handed them out. "They contain guidelines for your preparations. We'll leave the Academy grounds by shuttle at oh seven hundred next Monday, then transfer to the *U.S.S. Ajax* for the remainder of the journey. Any questions?"

Zhu shifted uncomfortably in his chair. "Sir, how extensive be the Arunu dig?"

"Quite extensive. Professor Spinaker's team has already exposed five square kilometers of a major city. I've included more information in your packets," and she indicated the data padds. "If there are no further questions, you are dismissed."

During their walk back to the dorm, Data tried to

engage Zhu in conversation, but the Tangonese gave only short, clipped responses. Clearly he didn't feel like talking. So Data decided to log his thoughts about the briefing in his journal.

Dear Diary,

Today I met the other members of my field trip team. Cadet Ejay Fantico would appear to be a competent leader, despite the comment from Lukas Whitlock that she looked anxious. Lukas himself is very open and friendly. I look forward to working with T'Pira, whose logical assessment of the dig operations should be most illuminating.

I wish to mention, however, that Zhu is still unhappy with our assignment. I can only hope that he will find something positive in the experience.

Sincerely,
Data

CHAPTER

3

The day of departure arrived. Data and Zhu met T'Pira and Lukas on the way to the Academy's shuttle field, so they all arrived as a group to find Cadet Fantico waiting. "Stow your gear and let's get going," she said. Before long, their shuttle was in the air.

Twenty minutes later, the *U.S.S. Ajax,* an Apollo-class starship in orbit around Earth, received the shuttle's occupants, then headed out of the solar system at warp speed, bound for Arunu. The planet wasn't particularly far from Earth, but it was located far from normal space lanes. Few starships traveled near the Karei System, because it had neither inhabited planets nor any planets with valuable resources. It had always been considered barren and worthless.

Until the discovery of the Arunuan ruins.

When the *Ajax* arrived at its destination, the cadets beamed down alone. As Data first stood on the planet's sterile soil, he felt as if he'd been there before. The desolate gray horizon reminded him of Omicron Theta, the planet where he had been found three years previously by the crew of the *U.S.S. Tripoli.*

Like that of Omicron Theta, Arunu's destruction was a mystery. Investigations revealed that it had once been lush with vegetation, and fossils from a variety of animal life had been found on every continent. Data wondered if the study of the ruins would eventually reveal the cause of the planet's demise.

"Kinda spooky," said Lukas, adjusting the transparent oxygen mask that covered his nose and mouth. One thin tube ran from the mask down to an oxygen canister attached to a specially designed belt. All the cadets wore such a device.

Data turned to Lukas. "Why should such a neutral landscape inspire fear?"

"It just does," Lukas replied, and shivered. "In fact, something about this place gives me the creeps."

T'Pira absently ran a hand up and down her arm, as if to rub down goose bumps. "At times I find Lukas's imaginative assessments illogical, but in this instance, I must agree with him. I, too, feel . . . disturbed."

"Perhaps it be a warning," Zhu murmured nervously.

Data placed his hand on Zhu's shoulder, a gesture he often saw humans make when attempting to reassure others. "There is nothing amiss here, Zhu. Perhaps you are imagining it."

"Maybe," Zhu responded, but he didn't sound convinced.

Ejay Fantico, who had been standing some distance away, joined the group. "I just reported in to the *Ajax*. She's leaving orbit now. Captain Benoi contacted Professor Spinaker, who should be here any minute."

Data noticed that even her voice held a note of apprehension. It looked unpleasant to be so disturbed, but Data couldn't help wondering what it felt like. "May I inquire why the professor requested that we beam down so far from the archaeologists' camp?" he asked Fantico.

"I don't know, Data, but he was specific about it."

T'Pira suddenly pointed east. "Someone is approaching."

From over a distant hill Data saw a cloud of dust. Seconds later a dirty gray vehicle topped the rise and floated swiftly toward them. The hovercar was an old open-topped model. Its quaint whirring electric motor made Data think of a giant purring cat. "Cadet Fantico? Hello! I'm Professor Jeffrey Spinaker," called a sandy-haired man, bringing the vehicle to a hovering stop. Even through the dust coating Spinaker's oxygen mask, Data could see the man's smile as he hopped out, along with two other people. All three of them wore masks, faded blue work tunics, and heavy boots.

Fantico shook Spinaker's hand. "It's a pleasure to meet you, Professor. These are cadets T'Pira, Lukas Whitlock, Zhu Lniuhta'bihd and Mr. Data."

Spinaker shook hands with each of them, trying not to stare too obviously at Data. The android recognized the expression, a combination of fascination and caution that many people wore upon meeting him. Data had never understood how two opposing emotions could mix so easily on the human face, but it certainly seemed a common phenomenon. "I am most pleased to meet you, Professor," he said, attempting to quell any uneasiness the human may have felt.

Data's efforts proved unnecessary. Spinaker grinned and shook Data's hand with a firm grip. "And we're very pleased to have you here." He gestured to the group. "All of you. As you might guess, we don't get many visitors. New faces are a welcome sight indeed."

He then introduced his colleagues, a tall, powerfully built man named Professor Lincoln Tesh and a small but sturdy woman named Dr. Jing-wei Ching.

"We're associates on the Arunu project," said Tesh. "Everyone else is at the dig."

"Hop in," Spinaker said, as Tesh hefted the cadets' duffel bags and placed them in the hovercar's cargo compartment. "Annie will get us there in no time."

Data cocked his head. "Annie?"

Dr. Ching laughed, patting the vehicle. "Yes. Arunu Annie. You'll find that most machines in the camp have names, Mr. Data. It gets lonely out here. Even inanimate objects become friends."

The cadets piled into Annie's back seat as the archaeologists squished together in the front. "Everybody wedged in nice and tight?" Spinaker asked jovially. "Then let's go!"

Annie took off over the barren soil like a Thoroughbred racehorse eager to reach the finish line. Data wondered if Spinaker always drove like a madman, but the other two archaeologists seemed to enjoy it. The cadets just hung on.

"So tell me," Spinaker called back as he drove, "how are you all feeling?"

The cadets exchanged nervous glances, then Fantico answered, "I think we're all excited, sir—except for Data, of course."

"Well," said Spinaker, "the Arunu dig is an unusual site. Newcomers always get the jitters. That, by the way, is why I asked you to beam down such a long distance away. It's better to approach the site gradually. When we get there you'll find out why. Just don't worry if your feelings become intense. They'll settle down soon." And with those mysterious words, Spinaker turned back to his driving.

Within moments the archaeologists' camp appeared in the distance, a cluster of weathered buildings nestled against the side of a steep hill. "At night the winds from the north can get pretty bad," Spinaker told them. "We situated the camp to the south of the tallest hill we could find near the dig." They zoomed past the camp and raced down into a shallow canyon.

Spread out like a map below lay the only known ruins of the Arunuan civilization, a checkerboard of sectioned-off squares about four meters across, each square in a different state of excavation. Data could distinguish portions of buildings, walls, doorways, and fragments of what looked like roads. Sections of ancient desks and chairs and other furniture poked out, half exposed, from the dirt, while metallic fixtures gleamed in the muted sunlight. The archaeologists had set up work tables in each square that were piled with smaller artifacts, most of them still partly encased in earth.

Spinaker brought Annie to a jolting halt. "How are you feeling now?"

Data was surprised when none of the cadets responded. Spinaker's driving hadn't been enough to alarm them this much. They looked more as if they were caught in a trance. Then T'Pira blinked and, barely maintaining her stoic expression, said, "Our sensations of unease originate from this site. Can you explain this, Professor?"

Spinaker and his colleagues hopped out of Annie, followed more slowly by the cadets. Data watched his peers with curiosity and concern. "Our greatest discovery about the Arunuans is their form of communication," said Spinaker. "Their culture was based entirely on emotion. Not the kind of emotion that you and I are familiar with—I'm talking about a pure, directed form of psychic energy."

"Everything you see here," said Tesh, "the walls of buildings, the tools, the machines, the art, every physical artifact on this site transmits a brief emotional impression when touched. As yet we have no idea how or why, but what you're feeling are the collected, residual vibrations of that energy on a subconscious level."

Try as he might, Data could feel nothing. "So the Arunuans did not speak aloud?" he asked.

"We're not positive of that," Dr. Ching replied, "but evidence suggests that they were mute. We've only found fragments of skeletons, far too little to theorize about their body structures."

At the mention of finding skeletons, Zhu cringed. Spinaker noticed. "Are you all right?" he asked.

"I be fine, sir," Zhu said hurriedly. "I just be . . . nervous."

Spinaker watched Zhu for a moment longer, then nodded to himself as if reaching a decision. "Starfleet Academy has asked me to give each of you an assignment while you're here." From his jacket pocket he produced a data padd and handed it to Fantico. "These are my suggestions, which you may give your team when you feel they're ready," he told her. Then he continued to the group, "But for now, why don't you all try to relax and get used to the place? Wander around, ask questions if you like, but I'd suggest refraining from touching anything until tomorrow. Somebody will drive you back to camp in an hour or two." With a wave, Spinaker left to go back to work.

Fantico activated the data padd she'd been given. "I think I'll give your assignments now. It might be helpful for you to observe the activities you'll be doing tomorrow." Consulting the padd's screen, she said, "T'Pira, you've been assigned to help log artifact statistics. Zhu, you'll be assisting one of the diggers in Section Seven. Lukas, you're assigned to the equipment crew. And Data—" Fantico paused, studying the data padd's screen. "Well, it says here that you're to study the site."

"Exactly what will I be studying it for, sir?" Data asked.

Fantico shrugged. "It doesn't say. You'd better ask Professor Spinaker."

Spinaker was already gone, perhaps down in one of the deeper excavation sections or in one of the work tents nearby. When Fantico dismissed the team, Data started walking to the nearest tent. "Data, wait!"

The android stopped and turned around. "Yes, Zhu?"

"May I—" Zhu paused awkwardly. "Um, never mind."

"May you what?" Data prompted, recognizing that the Tangonese was uncomfortable.

But Zhu just shook his head, forcing a smile. "No, never mind. I be okay." And he briskly walked away.

For a moment Data didn't know what to do. Zhu had appeared anxious, but now his walk appeared quite confident. Data concluded that he was all right, so the android resumed his search for Spinaker.

He found the professor in the first tent talking to Dr. Ching, who sat at a table filled with tiny fragments of what looked like plastic. Data stood politely at the entrance until Dr. Ching noticed him. "Why, Mr. Data, come in."

Data did so. "I apologize for the interruption, Dr. Ching, but I would like to ask a question of Professor Spinaker."

"Ask away," Spinaker said. "We were just trading cake recipes."

Data simply looked at him, waiting for some kind of explanation for the strange remark. When none came, his eyes darted to one side, a reflex that occurred whenever he made an extensive search of his memory banks. In this case, he was searching for all references that linked archaeology with baking. There were no matches.

The sound of Dr. Ching's laughter brought his conscious mind back. "That was a joke, Mr. Data," she said, and then to Data's surprise she punched Spinaker in the arm. "Be nice, Jeff."

Spinaker just grinned. "Data, I'll bet you want to ask me about your assignment."

"Yes, sir, I do. How did you know?"

"Because I left it vague on purpose. I wanted a chance to explain it to you myself. Mr. Data, I've been informed that your memory banks contain detailed cultural files from species throughout the Federation. I was hoping," and Spinaker gave a casual little wave of his hand, "to take advantage of your presence, frankly."

Data didn't follow. "In what way, sir?"

"Well, I'd like you to just look at things. Compare what you see to other similar items you may have stored in your memory. You have the unique ability to serve as a walking database, taking in information from the dig site and comparing it with your cultural files right on the spot. I'd like you to use your unique insight to form theories about Arunuan architecture, about their machines, about their art, about whatever you can think of."

Now that he understood it, Data was very pleased with his assignment. "A most challenging endeavor," he said. "I shall do my best."

Striding back out into the murky sunlight that constituted an Arunuan day, Data surveyed the dig site. His fellow cadets were wandering about, exploring their new environment. Watching them, Data suddenly understood the clever reasoning behind this field trip and why his xenoethnography instructor had specifically assigned his team to Arunu.

Being a Vulcan, T'Pira would find the emotional overtones of the site unsettling. She'd been assigned to Arunu so that she could exercise her Vulcan training and learn to tolerate emotional input when duties required. Zhu, whose Tangonese culture revolved around ancestor worship, found the very idea of an archaeological dig disturbing. No doubt he was on Arunu because his future Starfleet duties would require him to tolerate

activities that might contradict his strong beliefs. Lukas had no doubt been assigned to Arunu because he was interested in hostile environments. He'd mentioned to Data that, as an engineering major, he wanted to specialize in designing equipment to help people survive in harsh conditions. Data's own presence was obvious—he had no emotions. The study of a culture so steeped in emotional behavior was going to be an important part of his training.

While one section of Data's positronic brain continued to watch the activities around him, he accessed his internal memory banks and opened his file labeled Journal.

Dear Diary,

I am constantly amazed at how perceptive the human mind can be. After considering my assignment and those of my teammates, I now realize their significance. Each of us has been placed in a situation designed to force us to confront and strengthen our weakest characteristics. I assume the other xenoethnography teams have likewise been placed in such situations.

This serves as further proof that my decision to join Starfleet was a sound one. I look forward to learning much during this field trip.

Sincerely,
Data

Having made his journal entry, Data wondered how he should begin his assignment. He spotted T'Pira at the far end of the dig site studying several statues lined up on a rickety work table. Data decided to join her.

"What are these objects?" he asked as he approached.

T'Pira didn't answer. Data presumed she was deep in thought, probably analyzing the statues' strange abstract designs. Although they looked different from one another, there was a thread of similarity among them, something that Data couldn't quite pinpoint. Deciding not to disturb T'Pira, Data walked over to a storage shed where more of the objects were piled in boxes outside the door. Whatever the objects were, the Arunuans had created a lot of them.

Data tapped on the storage shed door. "Excuse me. May I enter?"

No one answered.

Slowly opening the door, Data peeked in and saw an amazing sight: rows and rows of shelves filled with more of the objects, but these had been cleaned. They were dazzling in the overhead lights, a riot of clashing colors, from deep blues and reds to the faintest, most whispered greens and yellows. Some had metallic trim, some were decorated with glittering gems, and still others bore markings that might have been some form of written language. Most of them stood at a height of about eight inches, but a few were as tall as two feet. Some were the size of a finger.

Data recalled Professor Spinaker's warning about not touching anything until the following day. The android wondered if that warning actually included him. After all, without the capacity for emotions, what danger could the objects pose to him?

He reached out a hand to touch one . . .

CHAPTER

4

Slap!

Data jerked his hand back and, whirling around, found himself facing three tall, frost-white humanoids. Amazingly, he hadn't heard them enter.

It was difficult to tell what their bodies looked like because of the long, loose robes they wore, but Data thought their heads resembled the Earth insect called a praying mantis. Sitting atop long, thin necks, their skulls were triangular in shape, hairless, with large eyes, tiny mouths, and no nose. What Data could see of their skin resembled polished white leather. One of them held a bony hand partway extended—he must have been the one who had slapped Data's hand from behind.

"Forgive me," Data said. "I should have asked permission before touching—"

"Tsidi," snapped one of the creatures in a thin, tinny voice.

Data searched his memory banks but could not find any translation for the word. *"Tsidi?"* he repeated. "Is that your name?"

Another of the creatures waved a long, thin arm at the objects all around them. *"Tsidi.* They are dangerous. We did not want you to become emotionally damaged."

"Do not touch them," warned the third creature in a low hiss, tilting its head at an extreme angle that would have broken the neck of any human. Its bulbous eyes had no lids, so it stared without ever blinking.

The eerie aliens didn't disturb Data in the least. "I do not believe the *tsidi* can affect me," he told them pleasantly. "You see, I have no emotions."

Neither, it seemed, did the strange white aliens. Their expressions hadn't changed once during the conversation, and their eyes lacked a certain sparkle that Data noticed in most intelligent beings. Were these creatures machines, as he was?

"Ah, I see you've met our Dyrondite associates."

The three Dyrondites swiveled their heads all the way around to look at Spinaker standing in the doorway behind them. No other part of their bodies moved, just their heads. Such a sight would have startled anybody but Data, who only found the creatures' insectoid behavior fascinating. Spinaker walked from the doorway to Data's side, and the aliens' heads slowly swiveled back around as their eyes followed him.

"I saw you head this way, Mr. Data, and thought I ought to formally introduce you," the professor said. "This is Scientist Pon Shaab, Scientist Pon Dbeq, and

Scientist Pen Sziid, representatives of Dyronda. Scientists, this is one of the Earth cadets, Data. He is an android."

Data expected the creatures to react the way everybody else reacted upon meeting their first android, but the Dyrondites didn't seem to care. The one called Pon Shaab said, "Acknowledged," and then all three turned their backs and walked outside.

Data blinked. "Did I do something wrong?"

"No no, that's just the way they are," said Spinaker. "Like you, Data, the Dyrondites have no emotions. They're the only species known to be completely psi-blind. Because of that, their idea of courtesy leaves something to be desired. What they lack in social grace, however, they make up for in intelligence and drive. They're a remarkable people. The Scientists have been invaluable to this project, since they're the only ones who can safely handle the *tsidi*."

"You mean these statues?" Data asked. "What exactly are *tsidi*, Professor?"

Spinaker scratched thoughtfully at the stubble on his chin. "Because of their decorations and the fact that they contain unusually strong emotional impressions, we think they're art objects. There seem to be two kinds, small ones we call *tsidi*, and the larger ones, which we call *tsidi* batteries. We found out the hard way that the batteries are dangerous. Even after four hundred thousand years, they still contain incredibly strong emotional impressions, so strong that species possessing emotions can't touch them without risking psychological damage." He sighed. "One of my best scientists, and a good friend, ended up in intensive care when he found the first bat-

tery. No one but the Dyrondites has touched them since." With visible effort Spinaker rallied his good spirits again. "But you, Data? Well, go ahead, touch one."

Perhaps he should have been cautious, but curiosity got the better of Data. He reached out to touch the surface of the *tsidi* he'd attempted to touch before, a battery about two feet tall, shaped something like a big twisted flowerpot, colored a deep blue and accented with delicate gold patterns.

The tip of Data's index finger made contact. Nothing. He lay his palm flat against the cool, porcelain-like surface. Nothing. Almost disappointed, Data picked up the battery with both hands. Nothing. "Excellent!" crowed Spinaker. "You can assist the Dyrondites if you like, then. I believe these *tsidi* are something important, but so far we can't tell what role they played in Arunu culture."

"I am at your disposal," Data said, carefully lowering the battery back to the floor, "but will my involvement disturb the Dyrondites?"

"Nothing disturbs the Dyrondites," Spinaker assured him. "It's logical for you to participate, so they'll be glad, so to speak, to let you participate. Their way of thinking is completely practical."

Data was fascinated by the idea of an entire culture that based its decision-making processes solely on an advantage/disadvantage basis. Like machines, Dyrondites behaved according to their circumstances, not their feelings about those circumstances. As far as Data was concerned, their way of thinking made more sense than that of humans or even Vulcans. However, after experiencing their cold greeting, Data decided that he still preferred the company of humans.

A scream from outside interrupted his thoughts. Data instantly identified the voice. "T'Pira!" He rushed out of the storage shed to find T'Pira as she had been when he'd last seen her, standing before a row of *tsidi* lined up on a work table. What he hadn't noticed before was the *tsidi* battery under the table. T'Pira's eyes were locked wide open and focused on it, her mouth still open from screaming, her body rigid.

Then she collapsed.

With superhuman reflexes, Data sprang forward and caught her before she hit the ground. "Water!" Spinaker barked to a nearby workman, and the fellow dashed off to the supply shed. "Was she touching the battery?" Spinaker asked Data worriedly. "Did you notice if her hand was reaching for it?"

"Both hands were at her sides," Data reported, gently laying T'Pira on the ground. "Besides, I do not think T'Pira would have touched the *tsidi*, sir, even if she were sure that it was safe. You suggested that we not touch anything today." A flicker of uncomfortable energy stabbed at Data's consciousness. His ethics program reminded him that he had almost done that very thing. He resolved to control his curiosity in the future.

The workman returned with a jug of water, and Spinaker sprinkled some on a cloth and pressed it to T'Pira's forehead. "No weapons," she was murmuring, as if in a trance. "Something else. Something . . ." She spoke so softly that Data almost didn't hear her. Then she snapped wide awake. "I am fine now."

Data helped her sit up and Spinaker offered her the water jug. "What happened?" the professor demanded.

"I did not touch anything," T'Pira hastily declared. "I was looking at those artifacts and then my attention was drawn to that large urn under the table. Before I knew it, my mind was locked on some kind of—" She groped for the word. "Frequency. Waves of violent, black emotions surged into me. I could not break away." She trembled, fighting to keep her Vulcan composure.

Spinaker was glaring at the *tsidi* battery. "Pon Shaab!" he snapped. "What is that battery doing out in the open? I gave you strict orders to keep them inside!"

Data watched as Pon Shaab, apparently the lead Dyrondite scientist, stepped forward. "This specimen requires more cleaning," he said in his neutral, raspy voice. "Pen Sziid does not place *tsidi* in the storage shed until all cleaning procedures are complete."

Spinaker calmed down. The explanation seemed reasonable. "Well, just be aware of our guests from here on, please."

"Yes, Professor."

"What happened?" Cadet Fantico and the rest of the Starfleet Academy team came running up, accompanied by Dr. Ching.

Lukas knelt down by T'Pira. "You okay?"

"I am fine, Lukas," T'Pira said, and again explained what she'd experienced.

"This has never happened before," Dr. Ching said worriedly. "I'm in charge of the storage units. If I'd had any idea such mental contact was possible, I'd have kept this unit locked."

"Doctor, there's no reason to blame yourself," said

Fantico. "If batteries are as powerful as you say, perhaps it was T'Pira's natural telepathic gifts that lured her into a mind-lock with that thing. At least we know to stay away from them now."

T'Pira struggled to stand, but Spinaker gently motioned her to stay put. "What I find puzzling," he said, "is that the few negatively-charged objects we've found so far have never relayed violent emotions without direct contact. Many of the *tsidi* batteries are negatively charged, but unless touched, they only create a vague sense of uneasiness." He looked questioningly up at Pon Shaab.

"We have only the ability to measure the intensity of *tsidi* energy output," the Dyrondite stated, "not the quality of the emotions. The batteries, such as that one, we have been unable to explain." He pointed a bony white finger at one particular section of the dig. "Section Twelve has contained more batteries than other sections."

"And Section Twelve hadn't yet been excavated when the telepaths were here," said Dr. Ching.

Data turned to her. "Telepaths?"

"I tried using the talents of various telepathic races to study artifacts, especially the *tsidi*," explained Spinaker, "but none of the telepaths could make sense of the impressions they received. I even invited the Vulcan Kolinahr Masters to come as well, hoping that their total mastery of emotion might help unravel the mystery. I guess the idea of an intense emotional experience didn't appeal to them."

"It would not," T'Pira confirmed.

"Then you're the first of your race to experience a

tsidi, Cadet T'Pira." Spinaker stood. "Data, if you would?"

It took a moment for Data to figure out what Spinaker wanted. Then he saw how weakly T'Pira moved as she tried to get up. He bent to help her but she impatiently waved him away. "I can stand," she said, barely struggling to her feet.

"Data," said Dr. Ching, "why don't you take her to Dolly's Bar and Grill, that building over there," and she pointed. "It has a controlled environment. T'Pira can take off her mask and relax."

Data was about to ask who Dolly was when he remembered Arunu Annie. This was probably another case of naming an inanimate object, he decided, in this case a whole building.

The interior of Dolly's Bar and Grill wasn't big. Four round tables with chairs, a portable replicator on a squat cabinet, and three cots filled almost all of its rectangular space. But once its inner door was sealed, T'Pira took off her mask and breathed deeply as if she'd just entered a fragrant garden. Data also removed his mask. He gestured T'Pira to sit, then ordered hot tea from the replicator. "Perhaps a warm beverage will help you recover," he said, handing her the steaming cup.

"Thank you." T'Pira sipped. Data was gratified to see her shoulders relax. She sighed. "Perhaps I should tell the professor what else I felt," she said, pronouncing the word *felt* with an inflection of distaste.

Data sat down next to her. "Your report was not complete?"

"It was, in the sense that I reported all facts. But of this one sensation I am not sure." T'Pira paused. "As my mind was caught in the storm of negativity, I sensed . . . destruction." She obviously didn't like her choice of words but could think of nothing better. "It was as if I could feel everything around me, all life, all that exists, simply gone in one instant. I think that's when I fainted."

"You mumbled the words 'No weapons. Something else,'" Data told her. "I do not believe anyone heard you but myself. What did you mean by that?"

T'Pira's eyes narrowed. "I do not remember saying it." Then she did something that Data had never seen a Vulcan do before. She shivered, but not because it was cold. The temperature in the room was maintained at a pleasant 22 degrees Celsius. "Something is wrong, Data," T'Pira said. "The *tsidi* are . . . wrong."

That night Data and his fellow team members settled into their camp quarters. They were assigned one large room with a contained environment, so their oxygen masks weren't needed. That, however, turned out to be the only luxury about the place. The walls were bare thermoplaster, and the floors were covered with thin synthetic carpeting. Five cots in a row against the wall, two tables, five chairs, and three mismatched lamps made up the furnishings. They had to go outside to a separate building to use the bathing facilities. "We run a Spartan operation," Spinaker told them with a wink. "Just think of it as your dorm away from dorm."

Fantico handed out files about the Arunu operation that Spinaker wanted them to read: bios of all the dig personnel, explanations of the equipment in use and the supplies available, the camp layout, the dig's source of funding—detailed background information that would be helpful when they began participation the following day. While they read, Fantico left to meet Professor Tesh in the communications hut to receive the cadets' homework assignments for that night.

Data scanned his file in less than thirty seconds. He wondered why it didn't contain much information about the three Dyrondites. It covered general information about their planet, as well as descriptions of some of the unique tools the Scientists were using at the site, but as for the race itself, all Data learned was that Dyronda was on shaky terms with the Federation. Being without emotions, Dyrondite politicians were considered by many Federation races to be rude, even brutal, and simple communication always led to arguments. The idea of polite manners simply didn't exist in their world. As yet they had seen no advantage to joining the Federation, and the presence of Scientists Pon Shaab, Pon Dbeq, and Pen Sziid at the dig was one of the few outreach efforts that had ever drawn the aliens out of their home system.

Most of the cadets were finished reading their files by the time Fantico returned. "Well, it looks like the comm system is out," she announced. "Professor Tesh is working on it, but he doesn't know what the problem is. He told me that if they can't repair it, Starbase Twenty-five will automatically send a ship to check on us in five days."

"Five days?" squealed Zhu. "We can't be gone that long! What about our other classes?"

"And all the homework?" added Lukas.

Fantico put her hands on her hips. "This kind of thing

can happen on a remote site, cadets. You know that. Handle it. That's what this training is all about."

"Ohhhh," Lukas said with a sly grin, "so that's it. A little test for us, eh? To see how well we deal with the pressures of isolation, eh?" He nudged T'Pira. "The comm system is out. Riiiiiight."

"I suggest you treat this as a real event, Mr. Whitlock," warned Fantico. "My report on your behavior and the reports submitted by Professor Spinaker will treat the matter as real whether it is or not. Even I don't know for sure."

With his grade on the line, Lukas straightened up. "Uh, aye, sir!"

Data held up his hand. "Excuse me?"

"Yes, Data?" said Fantico.

"I believe I can offer a solution to the classwork assignment dilemma. To satisfy my own curiosity, I recently downloaded all the textbook information required by every freshman-level class the Academy offers, as well as all suggested supplemental texts." Noting everyone's look of amazement, Data explained, "For me it is a simple matter of plugging into the Academy library network. If you wish, I can recite the lessons each of you requires."

"Well, I'll be," said Lukas. "You don't have to study, do you?"

Data was quick to correct such a misleading conclusion. "On the contrary, Lukas, I must study a great deal. However, much of what I need to learn is different from what the average cadet has to study."

Data noticed how relaxed the cadets were now as they focused on the situation at hand. He made no mention of it, but the emotional energy radiating from the ruins was affecting them less and less. Even Zhu appeared to be at ease.

The next hour passed with Data reciting class texts to each cadet. When he was finished, Fantico called lights out. "If you don't mind my asking," she said before turning out the last lamp, "what do you do at night, Mr. Data? You don't sleep, do you?"

"No, I do not. However, I have downloaded literary texts to study. At present I am engaged in a critical analysis of the complete works of the twentieth-century author Stephen King. I will be sufficiently occupied until morning."

The cadets said good night. As they drifted off to sleep in their bunks, Data sat at the table, silent and motionless, wondering how a "Pet Semetary" could bring dead people back to life.

CHAPTER

5

The next morning Data accompanied Fantico to the communications hut, only to be told that the comm system still wasn't operating. Data offered to help with repairs, but Professor Tesh told him, "I'm afraid the problem isn't down here, it's up there," and he nodded towards the sky. "All diagnostics reveal that our comm satellite isn't properly aligned anymore. I can't figure out why."

"So we get to wait five days until a ship comes," Fantico later reported to her team.

"Great," groaned Lukas. "This couldn't happen to us on Pacifica or Risa or someplace nice. No, we get five extra days in no-man's-land."

Fantico gave him a hearty pat on the back. "All the more time to live the life of an archaeologist. Put on your masks and let's get to it, people!"

Zhu stayed close to Data on their way to the dig site. The Tangonese was completely unnerved by his assignment, and as he had taken to doing since they'd become friends, he took comfort in Data's presence. "Since I am free to study the dig in any manner I choose, would you like me to assist you in your tasks this morning?" Data offered.

Zhu straightened up and gave his roommate a strained smile. "You be concerned for me. I be touched, Data, but no, I must do this myself. I be Starfleet now."

Mimicking Fantico's earlier action, Data gave Zhu a hearty pat on the back. "If I could feel pride, Zhu, I am sure I would feel some now."

As the cadets went to work, Data headed for the *tsidi* storage unit. After T'Pira's mishap, he wanted to study the batteries, plus he was curious about working with the Dyrondites. Never before had he met creatures so like and yet so unlike himself.

He found two of the aliens, Pon Dbeq and Pen Sziid, seated outside the storage unit, cleaning *tsidi* with a variety of gentle cloths, brushes, and solvents. As Spinaker had predicted, they accepted his presence. However, when he asked them questions about the *tsidi* they gave only short replies. After several such replies Pen Sziid said in her flat, tinny voice, "Refrain from further disruptions, cadet. We are working."

So Data offered to help them with their work. Instead they sent him off to get more cloths. Data obeyed, but when he returned with the cloths they sent him off to get more solvents. He got those, but when he returned they ordered him to go all the way back to camp and pick up a piece of equipment they'd forgotten to bring.

Suspicious now, Data jogged to camp and located the equipment, something called a *teu qitm,* right where they said it would be. But when he got back to the storage unit, the door was locked and the Dyrondites were gone.

Data stood there contemplating the locked door. He could inform Spinaker about the Dyrondites' lack of cooperation, but he should probably lodge a complaint with Fantico first. Then again, who was he to complain at all? He was a guest. They, on the other hand, had work to do. Perhaps Spinaker was incorrect about Dyrondite logic. Data might be a logical choice to help them, but not if they didn't want help in the first place.

The android decided to check on Zhu. He found the Tangonese scrambling out of the deep pit of Section Seven, covered in dirt and scowling. Offering a hand, Data easily lifted him up and out. "How are your efforts progressing, Zhu?"

Washing his hands in a bucket of water, Zhu snapped, "My efforts be fine. I be fine. The Arunuan we just dug up be not fine."

Data's eyes widened. "You found a body?" He leaned over and saw Dr. Ching and another workman huddled together, examining something small and white.

"It's an incredible discovery," Dr. Ching said, trying to control her excitement. "There's almost a complete skull here!"

Zhu was still washing his hands. "I have disturbed an ancient sleeper," he muttered. "It be wrong. Now we be cursed!"

Data felt an idea spark in his positronic brain, and he knelt down next to his friend. "Zhu, did you touch the bones?"

Zhu cringed. "Yes."

"During contact, did you feel any impression that the ancient sleeper was angry at your intrusion?"

Zhu stopped scrubbing his hands. "I felt nothing," he admitted.

"Might it not be possible then," concluded Data reasonably, "that an Arunuan, who had the ability to communicate emotions through objects while alive, might also have the ability to communicate anger after death through his own remains if he wished? And that if you felt nothing from those remains, that the Arunuan might therefore have no anger to express?"

Sitting back on his haunches, his hands dripping soap suds, Zhu thought about Data's words. Then he chuckled. "You be a good friend, Data."

Now it was the android's turn to get help. He explained to Zhu about the Dyrondites' behavior. "Well, if the storage unit be locked, just ask Spinaker for the key," suggested Zhu.

"I could do that," agreed Data, "but it is clear that the Dyrondites do not wish me to participate in their work. Were I to open the lock, they might interpret the action as intrusive."

The two walked over to Dolly's Bar and Grill, where they both took off their masks and Zhu replicated a tall glass of Tangonese spiced water. After a long drink of it, he said, "If the Dyrondites be a practical race, Data, perhaps they don't want your help because they don't consider you useful."

"But I have the ability to perform many useful tasks."

"Yes, but the Dyrondites don't know that. To them, you be just a first-year cadet."

Data followed Zhu to one of the tables, where they sat down. "But how can I prove that I am useful if they will not allow me to do anything?" Data asked.

"Hmm. Well, what matters to them most?"

"I would presume their work with the *tsidi*."

"Then find some way to help them with the *tsidi*."

At a loss, Data could only repeat, "But how?" Then he remembered what was still in his hand, the Dyrondite's *teu qitm*. He'd forgotten that he was holding it. Apparently the instrument measured the energy contained in a *tsidi*, the psychic energy of pure emotion. Data had read about it in Spinaker's files the night before. It was vital to the Dyrondites' work.

The android's eyes darted to one side.

"What be you doing?" asked Zhu.

Data finished his memory search. "I have formed an idea based on your suggestion. You have been most helpful, Zhu. Thank you." With that, Data put his oxygen mask back on and left Dolly's Bar and Grill, heading straight for the equipment shed, or rather, Uncle Teddy's Tool Emporium. "Go get a tricorder from Uncle Teddy's," he'd heard one of the archaeologists say earlier. All the basic equipment needed at the dig was stored there, and Data found exactly the tools he needed. He settled down at a workbench and began to take the *teu qitm* apart.

Dear Diary,

The Dyrondite Scientists have a device called a *teu qitm*, which functions somewhat like a tricorder, except that it is specifically tuned to register emotions as a pure energy output. I have learned that the Dyron-

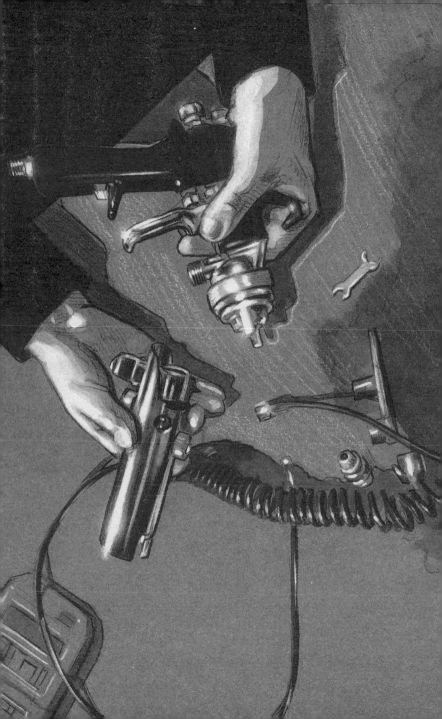

dite people invented these devices in order to interact with emotional species. It provides them with an indicator of what the other party is feeling, helping them gauge their responses for maximum benefit.

The *teu qitm* is allowing the Scientists here on Arunu to catalog the emotional intensity of the *tsidi* artifacts in an attempt to understand their function in Arunu society. If I can boost the device's sensing range, it will be more useful, not only for measuring *tsidi* energy output, but for locating more *tsidi* in other areas. If I am successful in this endeavor, perhaps the Dyrondites will be impressed enough to allow me to participate in their work.

Sincerely,
Data

By late afternoon, Data had indeed modified the *teu qitm*. Now it could register emotional energy over a distance of ten kilometers—over four hundred percent of its previous capacity—and its sensitivity was enhanced by nearly one hundred fifty percent.

At first, Data found Dyrondite technology to be something of a puzzle, but if there was one thing he had a knack for, it was machinery. He was satisfied with his tinkering and determined to show his creation to Professor Spinaker, as well as to the Dyrondites. After all, it could possibly help the archaeologists locate more Arunu artifact sites, which would please Spinaker and, in turn, benefit everyone.

Before showing anybody what he'd done, however, Data wanted to test his new device. Zhu, fascinated with Data's ingenuity, accompanied him. They hiked several kilometers from the dig site to the foot of a range of hills, and there Data activated the *teu qitm*. It accurately pinpointed the presence of *tsidi* at the dig storage unit, which it could not have done before at such a distance. It also identified the ornamental *tsidi* located in Dolly's Bar and Grill, plus the small *tsidi* that Spinaker displayed in an antique fishbowl in his camp office.

And then, in the opposite direction, far up in the barren hills, the *teu qitm* registered a huge concentration of *tsidi* energy underground.

CHAPTER

6

"Did you get permission to alter this device?"

Data answered his team leader truthfully. "No, sir."

He stood in the middle of a ravine halfway between the dig and the camp. That's where he and Zhu finally located Fantico, who had been on her way to camp for dinner along with the rest of the cadet team. The work day was over, and everyone was filthy and tired. Now Fantico was angry as well. "You surprise me, Mr. Data," she said sternly. "You of all people should know better than to take what's not yours."

"But it was already in my hand," Data insisted. "Besides, sir, it was the Dyrondites who left *me*. If I had been able to locate them, I would have requested permission to, as you put it, fiddle with the *teu qitm.*"

"Hmpf." Fantico examined the palm-sized device. "So you say you've improved this thing?"

"I believe so, sir. And I also believe that there is another cache of *tsidi,* or some kind of related artifacts, beneath those hills. The *teu qitm*'s reading was quite strong."

"If Data is correct, we should inform Professor Spinaker immediately," said T'Pira.

Lukas shook his head. "And if Data's wrong—no offense, Data—"

"None taken, Lukas."

"—then we'll all look like a bunch of losers. Maybe we should check it out first."

Fantico considered all their comments. "While I agree with T'Pira, I must admit that I agree with Lukas as well. I'd like to confirm Data's reading before announcing anything."

Data peered up into the cloudless grey murk of the Arunuan sky. The distant sun, a faint, blurry blob in the south, was starting to set. "There will not be sufficient daylight remaining to complete the journey."

"Then we'll go first thing tomorrow morning." Fantico decided that they'd all go, since it might prove educational. After all, they were there to learn.

The next morning before breakfast Fantico asked Professor Spinaker if they could borrow Arunu Annie for a quick trip. "Why do you want to go way out into the boonies?" he asked curiously.

"Data has made an . . . observation," Fantico answered, trying to be specific and vague at the same time.

"We'd like to check it out before jumping to any conclusions."

Spinaker's eyebrows crawled high on his forehead as he regarded his android guest. "I'll be interested to see what you're up to, Mr. Data."

"I, too, am rather curious, sir," Data replied honestly.

That made Spinaker grin. "All right, go ahead. But don't take Annie." He lead them to another hovercar, this one with a bulkier metal body and a much bigger electrical engine. "Let me introduce you to Bravo the Hover Bucket."

Lukas snickered.

"Hey, I didn't name him," Spinaker said, enjoying the cadet's amusement. "Some of the folks here are a little . . ." He twirled a finger near his ear. "Face it, archaeology is a form of madness. It takes a balance of smarts and pure lunacy to intentionally isolate yourself from all known civilization and spend every waking hour mucking around in dirt for rocks and bones. Get me?"

Fantico nodded. "Bravo will do fine, sir. Thank you."

Spinaker dug into a pocket and handed her the vehicle's activation card. "And be sure to talk nice to him. He runs better under encouragement." Giving them a wink, Spinaker turned and headed back to his office.

Data watched as Fantico tried to suppress laughter. She couldn't do it. "What a . . . *unique* individual."

"He's a loon," chuckled Lukas. At Fantico's sharp look he added, "But a nice loon. With authority over us. Sir."

The cadets piled into Bravo the Hover Bucket. Data kept the Dyrondite *teu qitm* firmly in his hand as Bravo rose two feet above the ground and soared over the landscape, its powerful hover jets blowing up great clouds of dust. The jets made so much noise that ten minutes later Data had to shout, "Here, sir!" when they arrived at the right spot. Fantico gently lowered Bravo to the ground. They were nearly five hundred meters from the base of the hills, with the camp almost four kilometers to the south, hidden by the smaller hill that protected it from the nightly northern winds.

Everybody piled out, and Data activated the *teu qitm*. Sure enough, it registered a large concentration of *tsidi*-like energy from deep beneath the hills. Following the signal, Data led the cadets closer until T'Pira said, "Over there, sir."

The entrance to the cave was tall, thin, and partially hidden by an outcropping of rock. It could easily have been mistaken for a shadow against the hillside. But T'Pira's sharp eyes had picked it out. Data could see it now, too, though the others had to move closer to make it out. "Mr. Data?" Fantico prompted, peering at the narrow opening.

Data held the *teu qitm* toward it. "The source of the reading comes from this direction," he confirmed.

Lukas and T'Pira, who both had been issued tricorders, activated the instruments. "Sir, something is limiting tricorder function," Lukas reported. "I'm not getting any clear readings."

"Confirmed," T'Pira said. "There is some form of strong interference. I am unable to pinpoint its origin, but clearly the tricorders cannot penetrate it."

Fantico hesitated for only a moment. "All right, people, we're just going in a few meters to see if there are ruins inside. Professor Spinaker will want to know."

The cadets nodded. Lukas fished around in Bravo's trunk and found two heavy-duty palm beacons. Fantico took one and told Lukas to keep the other. "You'll bring up the rear, Mr. Whitlock."

Zhu and T'Pira had no problem fitting through the cave's narrow opening, but Fantico, Lukas, and Data had to squeeze through inch by inch. Lukas scraped his head and shoulders when he got stuck and had to jerk himself through, and the back of Data's uniform tore when it caught on a sharp rock, but the cadets eventually made it inside.

The passageway widened once they moved past the opening. Lukas and Fantico lit their palm beacons to reveal its steep downward slope. Automatically lowering her voice to a whisper in the gloom, Fantico said, "Let's see where this goes. Data, take point." She handed him her palm beacon.

Taking the light, Data moved forward. For several minutes they walked in silence. The thin air grew cold as they descended, and the silence became so complete that Data thought he could actually hear the tiny internal hummings of his own systems.

It wasn't his systems, it was voices, far ahead. He switched off his palm beacon and stopped.

"Data, what—?"

Data waved his hand, cutting Fantico short. He peered into the darkness, then tipped his head slightly, turning his aural receptors up as far as they could go. "I hear voices," he whispered, "and there is a light ahead."

Lukas turned his beacon down to a soft glow. Data kept his turned off. Cautiously the group crept forward until the others could see dim flickerings on the walls ahead. A few more steps and the passageway made a sharp turn to open onto a large cavern. Data pulled back, motioning the other cadets to stay hidden.

Only Data had seen the three Dyrondites in the cavern, their tall white forms eerily lit by yellowish lantern light. The android didn't dare speak or the Dyrondites might hear him. Instead he slowly, silently turned his upper torso so that his companions could see his face. *Dy-ron-dites,* he mouthed as clearly as he could.

Everybody's eyes bugged.

"The carriers will load the cargo by hand," one of the Dyrondites said. At the sound of the voice so close and clear, the cadets automatically flattened themselves against the cave wall. "We cannot risk beaming. The dematerialization process might release the batteries' energy. The *Khemtk* will therefore land in the northern mountains, undetected by the camp without the satellite sensors, and send a surface transport here. Sziid, you will bring two batteries here early tomorrow, while the others consume first foods."

"Only two?" said another voice, Pon Dbeq, Data guessed. "We have so many."

"More than that will be missed," said the first voice. It must have been that of Pon Shaab. "The Ruling House is content to have two batteries and the smaller *tsidi* to study and make initial strike plans. We will provide them with more in the next shipment."

"How will the ship make it here a second time undetected?" Pen Sziid asked. "We cannot disable the satellite again without causing suspicion."

"That is my concern," was all Pon Shaab said.

Data glanced at his companions, who were exchanging

mute stares of shock. The Dyrondites had disabled the archaeologist's satellite communications! Data's modified *teu qitm* had led them right into the middle of what appeared to be a smuggling operation!

Fantico waved her hand, calling for attention. *Warn Spinaker,* she mouthed, and waved for them all to follow Lukas, who'd already begun to retreat. Data, who had been first in line, now cautiously brought up the rear.

"Might the Vulcan be useful?" Pen Sziid's query could still be heard as the cadets crept away. "She revealed this opportunity. Perhaps she can learn more for us."

"She is a child," Pon Shaab replied. "She only provided a demonstration of what we already suspected."

"The android?"

"He is a machine. His loyalty to Starfleet is no doubt programmed, making him useless for our purposes." There was a shuffling sound from the cavern—boxes being moved, Data concluded as he stepped carefully through the darkness. "These, however, will make the Federation loyal to *us.*"

Suddenly Data heard a shuffling sound *ahead* of him. One of the cadets must have slipped. They all froze in terror as Pen Sziid's tinny voice snapped, "There was a noise."

"Lukas, T'Pira, run!" Fantico whispered urgently. "We'll cover you!" Lukas and T'Pira dashed away as Fantico ordered, "Data, Zhu, show them you're unarmed."

Obediently, Data held out his empty hands and turned to face the Dyrondites, who rounded the far corner of the passageway and stared at the cadets with bland expressions. Apparently, Pon Shaab didn't notice that Data

was unarmed, or he didn't care. He calmly raised a disruptor. "Data, look out!" Fantico yelled.

But there was nowhere to go. A blast of light filled the passageway and Data felt a hot bolt of energy strike the middle of his chest. His limbs froze and he slammed to the ground, a high-pitched electronic squeal ripping through his circuits.

Then everything went black.

CHAPTER

7

*Dear Diary . . . Dear Diary . . . Dear Diary . . . Dear
Diary . . .*

Data slowly became aware of the internal voice—his
own voice—skipping over and over the beginning of his
most recent journal entry. As the android's various control programs rebooted, the circuit pathways of his neural net cleared. Within seconds he was able to silence
the internal voice and close his journal files.

Seconds after that his motor coordination returned.
He could sense that his body lay horizontal on a cold
rock slab. His eyes, frozen open but sightless, suddenly
accepted input again, and total blackness was replaced
by the figures of Zhu, Fantico, Lukas, and T'Pira kneeling around him, staring down into his face with worry.

"He's okay!" Zhu sighed with relief.

Fantico offered Data her hand. The android needed no help to sit up, but he accepted her hand anyway, having learned that humans were often insulted if their help was refused. "The Dyrondites fired an energy weapon that overloaded my neural net," he reported. "However, I do not believe I am permanently damaged."

"Good," Fantico told him, "because we may need some brute strength to get out of here."

Data glanced around. Stalagmites. Stalactites. Cave walls. No openings. Further scrutiny revealed that the Dyrondites had taken the cadets' commbadges, tricorders, and the modified *teu qitm,* but they had in turn provided their prisoners with a single hand lamp that cast listless shadows on the craggy walls. Strangely enough, the aliens had also left a *tsidi* battery in the cave, the same one with which T'Pira had accidentally mind-locked. "I do indeed possess physical strength far greater than that of humans," Data told his team leader, "but even I cannot punch through solid rock, sir. It appears that we are trapped."

"Well, we'd better untrap ourselves real quick and warn Spinaker," Fantico said. "After you fell, the Dyrondites captured all of us—"

"None too gently," grumbled Lukas, massaging his bruised neck.

"They mean business," continued Fantico. "This smuggling operation of theirs must be worth a lot."

"Then it is no wonder they did not wish me to participate in their work," Data mused. "I would no doubt have noticed their secret activities."

"They cannot be professional thieves," T'Pira said.

"Spinaker would have checked their credentials before hiring them to such a sensitive dig site."

Data nodded. "I agree. I do not believe the Dyrondites came to the dig with the intention of stealing *tsidi*. They would not have known of the artifacts' power until coming here. It is more likely that they later recognized the opportunity and, lacking any sense of loyalty to Spinaker, seized it."

"You are intelligent, cadets."

The cadets peered up through the gloom to see Pon Shaab standing on a ledge high over their heads. The cave's only opening yawned through the rocks behind him.

Data gazed up at the ledge, then down at the ground.

"They made us climb down a rope," Zhu said, answering his unspoken question. "They, uh, just dropped you."

"A ship from Dyronda will arrive soon," Pon Shaab said, his words echoing through the cavern prison. "This operation marks a new dawn for the Dyronda state. To secure our plans, we have concluded that your deaths are necessary. Spinaker must not know of our activities." And with that, he left. Seconds later, the yawning exit to the cavern collapsed under a barrage of disruptor fire.

The cadets ran for the far end of the cavern, trying to shield their heads from the rain of rocks that fell from the ledge. Data dared a glance up and saw the ledge itself giving way. "Data, protect the *tsidi!*" screamed T'Pira, her voice filled with what Data recognized as terror. *A Vulcan terrified?* But there was no time to wonder. Data dived for the *tsidi* battery, which lay directly under the falling ledge. Curling his body around the fragile art piece, he rolled quickly to one side as the ledge crashed

to the cavern floor. Rocks struck his back and legs, and the android felt himself being buried alive, but he didn't dare let go of the *tsidi*. T'Pira's tone had convinced him that it was far more important than anyone knew.

The cavern's rumbling finally calmed. The ground stopped shaking. Data opened his eyes—blackness. He flexed the servos of his arms and hands and felt that the *tsidi* was still in one piece. With android strength he carefully sat up, knocking back a pile of debris and rocks. He was filthy but whole, as was the *tsidi* battery.

After vigorously shaking his head to loosen the dirt in his hair, Data assessed his condition. His body was undamaged, but even his android eyes could see nothing in total darkness. "Is everyone all right?" he asked, his voice thick from all the dirt in his mouth. He coughed and tried to spit it out, but the air was filled with dust and the minute he opened his mouth, more of it wafted in. His syntheskin tongue felt coated with gunk. It was only at that moment that he realized his oxygen mask was gone.

"Data," came T'Pira's trembling voice through the nothingness somewhere to his right. "I am over here. Cadet Fantico is next to me. I think she has lost her mask."

Data heard Fantico gasping for breath. Quickly he sifted through the debris with his hands until he felt his own mask, dirty but whole. Unclipping the oxygen canister from his belt, he blew hard through the tube to clear it, then crawled toward the gasping sounds. "Here, sir." He did his best to wipe the mask clean with his shirt, then he reattached the tube and carefully reached out until he felt Fantico's head. Gently he slipped the mask over her face. "Attach the unit to her belt," he instructed T'Pira.

"I cannot. I think—" T'Pira gasped. "—I think my arm is broken."

Data attached the oxygen unit himself, satisfied when he heard Fantico start to gulp in the fresh air.

"Data." T'Pira's voice was filled with both pain and alarm. "The *tsidi*. Is it—"

"Intact, though I do not fully understand your alarm, T'Pira."

"It must not be damaged," she said emphatically.

Zhu spoke weakly from somewhere to Data's left. "Data, I be all right, but Lukas be not moving."

"Do you both have your masks?"

"Yes."

"Where is the lamp the Dyrondites left us?" Data asked. "Can anyone find it?" As everyone felt around for the light, Data thought to add, "I suggest we keep our voices low. If the Dyrondites want us gone, it may be wise to allow them to think that we are."

"Here." A scraping sound came from Zhu's direction and something hard bumped against Data's arm.

"Thank you." Data took the lamp and examined it with his fingers. It seemed to be intact, having been constructed to endure rugged environments. Data felt for the pilot spark button, pressed it, and the instrument emitted a feeble glow that was far too weak to be of much use to the humans. But Data's visual receptors utilized every microwatt of it, allowing him to see most of the cavern through a grayish haze.

The cavern floor, previously one slab of rock, was now a jagged mess of boulders, broken rock formations, and dirt. Lukas had awakened, and Zhu was helping him sit up. The Texan looked pale and disoriented. Fantico still lay on the ground recovering, and T'Pira crouched nearby, cradling her broken right arm. Her calm features reflected inner pain.

"At least we are still alive," Data stated, attempting to cheer the group.

Lukas coughed. "Yippee."

"Data." It was Fantico, her voice shaky. "Thank you for saving my life. But are you absolutely positive you don't need your mask?"

"Sir, I can breathe this air for a considerable period of time without harm. You cannot. Please keep the mask."

Fantico sighed with relief. "Far be it from me to argue with the cold hard facts."

"I have found it a useless endeavor, sir." Data stood up. "We must search for an avenue of escape."

"How?" Lukas muttered dully. "There wasn't one before. Why should there be one now?"

"Besides," said Zhu, "the light be too dim. We can't see."

"Incorrect. I can see somewhat." Data moved about the cavern, running his hands along the walls.

"If the Dyrondites wanted to kill us," Fantico wondered, her breath still labored, "why didn't they do it quickly? They could have simply taken our masks, or used their disruptors. Why a cave-in?"

"I would speculate," answered Data, continuing to feel the walls, "that they wished our deaths to look like an accident. If our bodies were found without masks or with weapons' injuries, authorities would presume foul play. The Dyrondites clearly want us gone under mysterious

71

circumstances so that they can continue to smuggle—"
His hand, feeling for rock, suddenly groped empty air.
"I have found an opening. It appears to be large enough
for us to move through."

"It must have been created by the cave-in," said
T'Pira. "It was not there before."

Fantico struggled to her feet. "Let's check it out,
Mr. Data."

"Are you up to it, sir?"

"That doesn't matter. We can't stay here."

"True, but please allow me to go first." Curling his
fingers firmly around the base of the lamp, Data turned
sideways and squeezed himself through. The crevice was
several meters long and almost as narrow as the original
cave opening. Data had to turn his head to one side to
keep from scraping his nose and chin against rock, and
he had to stand on tiptoe for his feet to fit. Fantico had
to do the same, but in minutes they reached the end.
"We've found another tunnel," Fantico softly called
through the crevice. "It's big. Maybe it's a way out."

"You be not going anywhere without us!" Zhu whispered frantically from the other end.

Before Fantico could reply an ominous rumbling came
from the cavern. "I believe the others should evacuate
with haste," said Data. "The cavern is not stable."

"I think you're right," Fantico agreed. But when Data
started back through the crevice, she grabbed his arm.
"Where do you think you're going?"

"T'Pira is injured. Zhu cannot aid Lukas alone, and
you are still weak."

Fantico growled in frustration. "Well, take the light
with you, then."

Moving as quickly as he could, Data squeezed back through the crevice to find T'Pira and Zhu struggling to help Lukas stand up. Data now saw the gash across the side of Lukas's head. "Join Starfleet," the big Texan was mumbling. "See the universe. Ha!"

"He probably has a concussion," grunted T'Pira, trying to support Lukas with only one arm.

Data slipped his arm around Lukas's waist, easily holding the weight. "Go, T'Pira. Zhu, accompany her. I will handle Lukas." The cavern rumbled again, and more rocks fell. "I will carry the *tsidi* as well. Zhu, please take the lamp. I would advise that you depart with extreme haste."

T'Pira and Zhu were soon wriggling through the crevice to safety, leaving Data in darkness. Supporting Lukas with one arm, his other hand grasping the *tsidi* battery, Data half walked, half carried Lukas in the direction of the crevice. It took him a moment to find it without light. Just when he did, the cavern groaned and more rocks rained down, thumping to the ground far too close for comfort. "Hurry up!" Fantico called through the crevice.

"I am not sure if you can hear me, Lukas," said Data, "but if you can, stand up straight and maneuver sideways."

"Sure," Lukas mumbled agreeably. "No sweat."

As if he were walking in his sleep, Lukas sidled into the crevice, and Data squeezed in after him. There was barely enough room for the android to keep a grip on Lukas's arm and around Lukas's waist to steady him, and the *tsidi* barely fit through the narrow spaces, but they managed to proceed, however slowly.

Just as Lukas made it out the other end, the cavern behind them roared. Data scraped the rest of the way through at top speed, followed by puffs of thick dust and trickles of debris. "The cavern has collapsed," he announced as he emerged, his calm voice unable to communicate just how close they'd all come to death.

Zhu shivered. "Whatever. Let's just go."

"Agreed." Fantico handed the lamp to Data. "You're in the best shape of any of us. You lead."

Data took the lamp, his other hand still holding the *tsidi* battery. He assured T'Pira, "It is scraped but unbroken." She only nodded, so Data started forward, following the slight incline of the tunnel to his right, hoping that it would lead to the surface.

Dear Diary,

My teammates and I have stumbled onto what appears to be a *tsidi* smuggling operation on the part of the Dyrondite archaeologists. However, my memory records indicate that the Dyrondites want the *tsidi* for more than artistic or financial gain. Pon Shaab spoke of "initial strike plans," but against whom? And for what?

A ship from Dyronda, referred to as the *Khemtk*, will be arriving tomorrow to pick up the first of several *tsidi* shipments. Whatever their ultimate goal, the Dyrondites are willing to kill for it. My teammates and I must find a way out of these caves so that we can warn Professor Spinaker and Starfleet.

Sincerely,
Data

"It's been hours," groaned Lukas. "I gotta stop." Without waiting for a reply, he sank to his knees in exhaustion.

"We have been traveling for only one hour, twenty-six minutes, thirty-two seconds," Data informed him. "However, if you require rest, I am fully capable of continuing on my own."

Fantico nodded. "Then let's go. The rest of you, get some rest."

Leaving the *tsidi* battery behind with the others, Data and Fantico traveled several minutes before reaching a junction where the tunnel split into two. "Which way would you suggest, sir?"

Fantico didn't hesitate. "Right."

They entered the right-hand tunnel, but in less than a minute the passageway started to shrink. Soon they had to stoop to avoid hitting their heads on the ceiling. Then they had to drop to their hands and knees. Finally, even crawling wasn't enough; the tunnel squeezed itself into a dead end.

After awkwardly backing out, the two cadets returned to the junction. Automatically Data started down the left tunnel, but Fantico hung back. "I don't think we should go that way, Data."

"Why not?"

Fantico seemed confused. "I don't know. I just don't think it's a good idea."

Data held the lamp up, examining her expression by its faded light. He was hardly an expert on human emotions, but he recognized that look. It was the same look the cadets had worn when they'd first arrived on Arunu.

"Sir, are you aware that you appear to be nervous, just as you were when we first arrived on this planet?"

Fantico looked at Data in surprise. "You're right. The feeling just sort of crept up on me. There must be Arunuan artifacts in there."

"If so, sir, they must contain unusually strong impressions to affect you this way. Are you certain the others can handle it?"

"Well, we can't go all the way back to the cavern to try the other way. We just don't have the energy. We need food. We need water. T'Pira and Lukas need medical help."

"As do you, sir," Data reminded her. "Perhaps I should continue on alone, and report back what I find."

"Cold hard facts," Fantico muttered. "Okay okay, go ahead."

Data started down the other tunnel, but within minutes he hit another dead end. However, this one didn't look natural. It looked more like a manufactured wall. The android could see the faint outline of an archway in the rocks, and the fill material had a texture completely different from any natural rock.

Curious, Data hefted a large, sharp rock and hit the strange material. He hit it again. And again. After several strikes, some of it crumbled away.

"I may have found a way out, sir," he reported when he returned to the team. Fantico had groped her way back in the dark and was lying on the cold dirt with the others. Data flashed his light on Lukas, whose skin shone pale against the dark tunnel floor. T'Pira was shivering with fever.

After Data's explanation of his discovery, Fantico said,

"Even if you did pound your way through, Data, we don't know where it leads."

Data indicated T'Pira and Lukas. "I see no viable alternative, sir."

Everybody was too tired and weak to argue. Leaving them in darkness, Data returned to the archway with the lamp. Setting it down a safe distance from the wall, he hefted the sharp rock he'd used before and resumed pounding on the archway with all his android strength. He knew his comrades could hear each blow echoing through the tunnel, relentless, untiring, determined.

CHAPTER

8

Dear Diary,
  I have been attempting to break through the cavern wall for one hour, fifteen minutes, forty-one seconds. I think I may succeed in the next few minutes, though what I find within may or may not prove helpful. I am concerned that my teammates may not last our journey, especially Lukas and T'Pira, who require medical attention.

Sincerely,
Data

Data had barely finished his journal entry when his hand, which had been unceasingly and rhythmically pounding against the wall with the rock, suddenly broke through. He lost his balance as his whole arm disappeared into a hole.

Recovering, Data withdrew his arm and peeked through the opening. Beyond sprawled a huge cavern; its walls glittered with multicolored gems. Data could see no light source to create such glittering. The gems themselves seemed to glow from within.

Encouraged by his find, Data tore at the wall now, yanking whole chunks out with his bare hands. Before long he had a hole big enough to step through.

The first thing he noticed was that his feet landed on a floor mosaic composed of hundreds of perfectly interlocked stones, polished to a gleaming shine that reflected the gemlight all around.

The second thing Data noticed was that the gems weren't natural deposits. The cavern, bigger than the bridge of a starship, was filled with *tsidi* batteries, none smaller than three feet tall, many as tall as a man, and all of them decorated with gems of every size and shape.

The third thing Data noticed was that every battery was broken.

"I now believe the energy reading I detected with the modified *teu qitm* was not caused by the Dyrondite's stolen *tsidi*," Data said to Fantico, "but by the batteries in the cavern I discovered."

"They're all broken?" T'Pira, fighting her fever, shook her head. "I don't understand. They can't break. They *mustn't* break."

She'd said that before to Data without explaining what it meant. "Is this an impression you received during your mental contact with the battery?" he asked her. "Or are you making what is known as an educated guess?"

"I do not know." T'Pira fought to think clearly. "I only know I am right."

"In that case, sir, I would like to study the cavern further."

Fantico finally showed her temper. "Mr. Data, I commend your interest in archaeology, but we're in a bit of a bind here!"

Data remained unfazed. "On the contrary, sir, I was hoping that if the cavern was created by the Arunuans, perhaps there is another exit."

"Oh." Fantico paused. "You're right. I'll help Lukas and we'll follow along as soon as we can."

"Very well, sir." Data handed her the light and returned to the *tsidi* cavern, using his unerring memory to guide him through the pitch blackness. Once he reached the cavern, the glowing gems provided enough light for him to see.

One feature of the cavern intrigued him the most: a series of four large tapestries hung side by side against one wall. Woven from bright threads of some unknown material, the tapestries displayed symbols that Data suspected were words. He'd seen such symbols at the dig, carved into walls, some stamped into metal utensils and other artifacts. Several of them he recognized. He hoped that by running a comparative analysis of these symbols with similar symbols from other language files, he just might decode the Arunuan language and translate what the tapestries said. Hopefully the information would help their present predicament.

He was still in analysis mode when Zhu and Fantico

arrived. They stood in silent awe, taking in the splendor of the glittering cavern. Then Fantico said in a strained voice, "Data, we left T'Pira and Lukas back at the junction. The *tsidi* energy is too painful for them."

"Cadet Fantico and I can handle it, though," Zhu added with effort.

Data didn't move. "I am currently engaged in a complex analysis. One moment, please." Although most of his concentration was focused inward, Data was still aware of the cadets watching him curiously. Finally he turned to Fantico. "Analysis complete, sir. These tapestries are covered with word symbols. I believe they tell the story of why these *tsidi* batteries are here."

Fantico was struggling to maintain composure under the powerful *tsidi* energy swirling invisibly around them. "And?" she said with effort.

"I cannot be certain of my interpretation, but I believe these *tsidi* were created as ceremonial vessels into which the telepathic Arunuans projected their negative, violent emotions in some kind of cleansing ritual. I do not think they ever intended to return to this cavern, nor did they intend for anyone else to find it. It is, if I may so phrase it, a psychic dump. If these *tsidi* were intact, the concentration of so much negative energy would prove deadly. However, because they broke long ago, only faint traces of the energy remain, unpleasant but bearable."

"Why did they all break?" asked Zhu.

"Unknown. T'Pira seems certain that they were intended to remain intact."

Fantico shivered. "Good work, Data. Your discovery is dazzling. Now what good can it do us?"

Her sarcasm went right over Data's head. "The tapestry to the left shows an archway," he answered pleasantly, "and so does the tapestry on the right. I am hoping that means that another archway exists similar to the one I broke through."

"Then let's find it!"

Fantico, Zhu, and Data began to search. They'd covered almost the entire perimeter of the cavern and were beginning to get desperate when Zhu said, "Wait a minute—the tapestries!"

Data turned. "What about them?"

"Maybe the archway is behind them!"

Fantico groaned. "If you're right, I just may kick myself."

The three cadets struggled to loosen one of the tapestries from the wall, which was no small task since the heavy fabric had been attached with some kind of alien glue that had survived four hundred thousand years at full sticking power. But they only had to lift the bottom half of the thick material to see that an archway did exist, carved out of the cave wall and filled in with the same strange material that Data had first broken through.

Data searched the floor and picked up a large rock with a sharp end. "This will take some time, sir," he said.

Forty-six minutes later, Data stopped pounding. While he'd worked, he'd also been analyzing everything he knew about the Dyrondites, their planet and their behavior, comparing that information with recent events. A simple smuggling operation just didn't make sense. Pon Shaab and his associates wouldn't risk their professional reputations for mere money. Dyrondites took advantage

of opportunities, yes, but the risks of stealing *tsidi* were far too great to be offset by mere monetary gain.

Pon Shaab's words, "initial strike plans," nagged at him, and he suddenly realized what they were after.

The absence of Data's pounding sounds brought Fantico and Zhu running. "What's up, Data? Have you broken through?"

"Not yet, sir, but I think I may have determined why the *tsidi* are so important to the Dyrondites." Data's emotionless tone somehow conveyed a sense of alarm. "It is possible they will be used as weapons."

"What?" responded Fantico.

Zhu's jaw dropped. "Of course! Most species in the Federation be intolerant of *tsidi,* right? Even when whole. What if one be broken in a public place?"

"Death would result, theoretically on a grand scale," Data concluded. "All along T'Pira has warned us to keep the Dyrondites' *tsidi* battery intact. Perhaps her earlier contact with it gave her the subconscious knowledge of its true potential. That would also explain why Pon Shaab placed a battery in the cavern with us before causing the cave-in. He intended the cave-in to kill us all, and the *tsidi*'s remains would have provided an explanation for our deaths if our bodies were ever found."

Fantico gestured at the cavern. "So you're telling me that all these *tsidi* were broken on purpose?"

"No, not these," answered Data. "These were ceremonial, intended to keep their negative energy safely contained. But the other *tsidi* batteries found at the dig weren't in such a vault as this. Perhaps they were weapons."

"All the Dyrondites have to do be to break one bat-

tery in a key location within a city, or continent, or even a whole planet, and they could throw that government into chaos," Zhu murmured, stunned by the horrible possibilities.

"Pon Shaab did speak of initial strike plans," Data added, "and he said that the stolen *tsidi* would make the Federation loyal to the Dyrondites. By coordinating the placement of negatively-charged batteries throughout the Federation's power bases, the Dyrondites could conceivably disrupt the galaxy's entire political structure."

"Wait, wait, wait. Just hang on a minute." Fantico shook her head. "You two are flying way off into uncharted space here. The Dyrondites are definitely up to something, but galactic takeover is a bit much, don't you think? Dyronda isn't a member of the Federation, but its people have never caused problems in Federation space. They're not conqueror types."

"We do not know that for certain, sir," said Data. "They may never have had such an opportunity before. Consider." He gestured to himself. "I have a point of view that you do not. If my creator had not provided me with an extensive ethics program, I would be much like the Dyrondites: motivated by circumstances, judging my actions according to immediate advantage or disadvantage. I can understand how such a species, upon finding an opportunity to greatly benefit their planet, could consider mass murder to be a perfectly acceptable form of expansion, especially if the weapon used posed no threat to their own kind."

The three cadets fell silent, each of them imagining the same awful possibilities. Then Fantico snatched a rock up from the ground. "C'mon, Zhu. Let's help Data get this wall down!"

When they finally broke through, Data, Zhu, and Fantico found themselves facing another tunnel. This one sloped upwards at a steep angle. "Let's get the others and get out of this place," said Fantico.

Data carried Lukas through the *tsidi* cavern as fast as he could, trying to keep the human's exposure to the psychic energy as brief as possible. Fantico and Zhu helped T'Pira make a mad dash through, but even a few seconds in the cavern caused the Vulcan to double over in pain.

After another hour of uphill walking through twists and turns and a maze of stalactites and stalagmites, the cadets reached the surface of Arunu. The midnight moon welcomed them back, and the northern winds howled, eager to knock them over. Data's internal chronometer told him that twenty-two hours, seven minutes, and fifty-three seconds had passed since they'd left the camp. The archaeologists would have been forced to stop searching for them by now, but no doubt Spinaker would order the search to continue at first light.

If they'd had the energy, the cadets would have whooped for joy to be above ground once again. Instead they staggered around a low hill and, barely shielded from the wind, collapsed in exhaustion—all except for Data, who scanned the horizon. "I do not know where we are, sir, but I do not see Bravo the Hover Bucket. Without a vehicle you and the others cannot possibly make it back to camp."

"You go." Fantico tiredly waggled her hand. "Cold

hard facts, Data. You tell Spinaker what we've learned and tell him where we are. We'll hold out here until help comes."

Data nodded. "Aye, sir."

He took off at a dead run, and he kept on running all the way to camp.

CHAPTER

9

Spinaker sat on the edge of the table, staring suspiciously at the little *tsidi* that he'd kept in a fishbowl in his office for the last five months.

Data had made it back more than an hour before, reporting in detail everything that had happened. The other cadets had been rescued, and T'Pira and Lukas were now safely recuperating in the archaeologists' medical facility.

The camp, however, was in an uproar. Everyone had gathered in Gandy's Grubhole, the cafeteria building, where Spinaker sat before them trying to make sense of what he'd learned. "So this," he said, turning the *tsidi* over and over in his hands, "is nothing but a weapon." Regret filled his voice.

"No, sir, that *tsidi* is a decorative art piece," Data corrected him. "Only the batteries are weapons."

At first Spinaker had refused to believe any of Data's

story, not because he doubted Data's word, but because he couldn't accept that his archaeological expedition had produced a discovery that might very well tear the Federation apart.

He slid off the table and walked over to Pon Dbeq and Pen Sziid, who had been taken into custody and who now stood by the door, their bony wrists and ankles bound. When they learned that Data had returned, they'd tried to flee. That alone was enough evidence to convince Spinaker that the Dyrondites were indeed guilty. Still, it wasn't yet crystal clear what they were guilty *of*. "Why don't you just tell me what you were planning?" he asked them for the umpteenth time.

Tipping her strange mantis head so far to one side that she ended up looking at Spinaker sideways, Pen Sziid replied in her tinny voice, "Under present circumstances, it is not wise for me to speak." Pon Dbeq tilted his head the same way, as if such a gesture was a Dyrondite expression of resistance.

Data had never seen Spinaker angry before, and the change in the man was unsettling. Normally easygoing, even playful, Spinaker now trembled with suppressed rage, his eyes gleaming with a dangerous light. "The cadets can take us to your cave," he warned them. "I'm sure Pon Shaab is there. We can stop your little scheme right now."

"That is doubtful." Pen Sziid slowly, eerily tilted her head the other way. "The winds beyond camp are too strong for travel. Our ship will arrive tomorrow morning. Even if you capture Pon Shaab, even if you eliminate all three of us, you cannot stop a warship of the Ruling House, nor are you able to call for assistance from Starfleet. We will have the *tsidi*."

Spinaker turned his back on them. "Tesh, get them out of here. Put them in the Pit and post guards."

The Pit was the only underground facility in the camp. It was a large emergency room designed to shelter the entire dig staff from Arunu's two greatest threats—lightning storms, the likes of which had never been seen on Earth, and incredible windstorms, far more violent than the nightly northern winds. So far neither emergency had occurred, but the Pit stood ready just in case.

Now it would serve as a jail.

Tesh and two other diggers led their prisoners outside as the crowd anxiously murmured opinions. Fantico spoke up. "Professor Spinaker, you must have some kind of plan in case of an outside attack."

Spinaker shook his head. "This is a scientific establishment, not a battleground."

"We have—*had*—our comm satellite," said Dr. Ching, "and once a month a starship comes by. We thought that adequate."

One of the diggers, a petite black-haired woman, said, "Can we hide the *tsidi?*"

"Where?" asked Spinaker. "They took Data's modified *teu qitm.* They can find *tsidi* anywhere now."

"I regret creating such a complication," Data apologized.

"Are you kidding?" Spinaker laughed bitterly. "Data, if not for you, who knows how many *tsidi* batteries would have been smuggled out right from under our noses? No, we owe you our thanks for exposing this fiasco." He sat back down on the table. "We just have to figure out what to do about it."

More debate ensued, but the conclusion remained the same: even though the archaeologists had tools that could be used as weapons, they didn't have the firepower to challenge a starship, especially one loaded with armed Dyrondite War Guards.

"Wait a minute," said Fantico. "If we can't fight them, maybe we can trick them."

"How?" asked Dr. Ching.

"We've got a potential secret agent in our midst." Fantico pointed at Data. "Data is a lot like the Dyrondites. What if he convinced them he wanted to switch sides? They'd take him into their ship, presuming that he'd be leaving with them, right? Once inside, Data could sabotage their weapons or engines or whatever he can get hold of."

Everyone seemed to like the plan, but Data broke through the rising hubbub. "Excuse me, everyone, please." They all stopped talking. "I am afraid there is an insect in this particular ointment. My programming is not designed for deceit. I doubt whether I could successfully convince the Dyrondites that I have chosen to take their side. In addition, it is wrong to lie, is it not?"

Fantico put her fists on her hips. "You're a Starfleet cadet, mister. You'll do as ordered."

"That is not in debate, sir," Data replied, "but the fact remains that—"

"Sir?" Zhu stepped quickly up to his team leader. "If I may?" Fantico, curious, nodded to him. Zhu grabbed Data's arm, the way he always did whenever he wanted the android's full attention. "Data, think of it like your birthday party. I tricked you into coming to the study lounge, remember? I deceived you, but for a good purpose. This be the same idea. You've got to fool the Dyrondites and get onto their ship so you can stop them from eventually waging war on the Federation. Ruse be a basic combat strategy. It be part of what you be at the Academy to learn, right?"

Data quickly analyzed the two situations in relation to his ethics program. He was surprised to conclude that Zhu was right. "I think I understand," he said, amazed by this revelation.

Fantico nodded. "Good. Now all we need is some kind of explosive."

"The closest thing we've got are cobiem charges," said Dr. Ching.

The cadets had already learned that archeologists had stopped using explosives long ago when cobiem was discovered. An unstable element sensitive to sonic vibrations, cobiem could be used to create controlled vibrations through sand and rock, thus loosening artifacts from the earth without the time, cost, and manpower of standard digging methods.

"Cobiem," Spinaker mused, nodding his head. "Right. What are you going to do, vibrate them into submission?"

The archaeologists laughed nervously at the joke, but Fantico frowned. "No, Professor, but if put in the right place, say their engine room, its vibrations might disrupt their instruments so badly the engines won't operate. It might take out other control systems as well."

"But how can Data get a cobiem charge onto their ship?" Zhu asked. "The Dyrondites be not stupid. If they do let him aboard, they'll scan him first."

Spinaker heaved a frustrated sigh. "Well, so much for that idea."

"Not necessarily." At those words, everybody looked at Data. "How big is a cobiem unit?"

Dr. Ching made a fist with her hand. "It's in a box

about this big that's designed to amplify the cobiem's vibrations, but the actual mechanism is smaller than one of your commbadges. Even so, it's big enough to alert even the simplest scanner."

"Again, not necessarily." Lifting his arm, Data rolled up his sleeve. As everyone curiously watched, he tapped the syntheskin of his forearm and an access panel popped open, revealing a maze of circuitry and tiny blinking lights inside. "Perhaps I can hide the cobiem unit in this gap between the servos of my forearm. I will have to be careful not to use this arm while the device is there, but the Dyrondites should not be able to detect it."

"And if they do," Zhu said, "they'll think it be part of your own systems. Clever, Data! See, I knew you'd catch on!"

"Then you'll do it?" Spinaker asked hopefully.

Data nodded. "I will do my best."

Dear Diary,

After replaying my memory record of Pon Shaab's instructions to his fellow scientists in the cave, I have been able to determine the approximate landing site for the Dyrondite ship, *Khemtk*. I am now en route on foot to the cave where I and my teammates escaped. I will approach the *Khemtk* from that direction, so that the Dyrondites will think I alone have escaped their trap.

What I am about to do may save the Federation, as Professor Spinaker says, but I continue to debate whether or not I will succeed. The odds are not in my favor, yet I must try.

Sincerely,
Data

After jogging for twenty minutes, Data reached the cave where the cadets had emerged the night before. From that point he continued north, heading for the mountains but angling west so that he'd find the valley that Spinaker said would be the best place for a warship to land and remain concealed.

Fantico had told Data not to bathe or change his uniform, so that he'd look as if he'd just come from the cave-in. Glancing down at himself as he jogged, the android figured that his appearance, at least, would support the story he planned to tell the Dyrondites. He was a filthy mess. At Zhu's suggestion, Data had also discarded his oxygen mask. The more machinelike he looked and acted, the more the Dyrondites might believe his story.

Data had left camp before dawn. He reached the target valley just as the sun was beginning to rise. Sitting down next to a huge boulder, he waited, watching the shadowy pit of the valley slowly reveal its craggy, barren surface in the sun's growing light. He could only hope that this, indeed, would be the *Khemtk*'s touchdown point.

He didn't have to wait long. Less than an hour later he noticed a tiny dot of silver high in the sky. The dot descended, growing larger and larger until it resolved into a space ship. It was far smaller than Data had expected, maybe the size of a commercial warp shuttle, but its design spoke volumes about its purpose: this was a vessel of destruction, bristling with weaponry, sensor arrays, and heavy-duty deflector dishes.

Data waited until a ground transport appeared, presumably to travel to the cave where the stolen *tsidi* were waiting. It dropped down out of an open port in the ship's belly and gently lowered itself on hover jets to the

dirt. After it skimmed away, Data rose to his feet and began walking toward the main ship.

Before he'd gotten within shouting distance, a troop of seven-foot-tall, armored War Guards materialized around him, rifle-like weapons drawn, their bony, triangular faces without expression. "Identify," one of them commanded.

"I am Data. No doubt Pon Shaab told you about the Starfleet cadets who discovered your plans. I am—was—one of those cadets."

The War Guards took aim.

"Wait, I wish to join you!" Data said hastily.

"Explain."

Data gave his speech exactly as rehearsed. "While it is true that I first attempted to stop your plans, I have reconsidered my position. Every cadet but myself was killed in the cave-in arranged by Pon Shaab. As I dug my way out, I had time to analyze your people's philosophy versus that of the Federation. I find your methods of operation far more suitable to my programming and offer my services to your cause."

"You are the android?"

"Affirmative."

Without any signal that Data could detect, the War Guards all lowered their weapons. The only one to have spoken so far tapped a communications device on his armor, spoke rapidly into it, then slapped a small metal disc onto Data's shoulder that stuck fast to the fabric of his uniform. As Data was about to ask what it was, he felt the unmistakable sensation of a transporter beam grab him.

CHAPTER

10

Data started to rematerialize, but something stopped the process. Hanging in the helpless limbo of partial solidity, the android suspected he was being scanned. His suspicion was confirmed when the words, "Negative, Gil-Pon," drifted by.

Another voice, deep and equally empty of emotion, responded, "Very well."

The transporter finished reassembling the scattered atoms of Data's body, and he found himself standing on what he assumed to be the bridge of the *Khemtk*. While the ship itself had been smaller than he'd expected, the bridge was bigger than he'd expected. Five Dyrondite officers were at their stations, plus Data himself, two War Guards, and the captain in his center seat.

The captain stood up, towering a good two feet over

Data. "You will address me as Gil-Pon Ldaaq. You are aboard the warship *Khemtk*. You will retain your transporter tag."

Data realized that he meant the disc stuck to his uniform. "Very well, Gil-Pon Ldaaq. I am Data—"

"I know who you are and why you have come." The captain leaned over Data as if to intimidate him, tipping his mantis-head so that one bulging eye stared down into Data's upturned face. "Explain how it is possible for an android programmed by Starfleet to reject Starfleet."

"I was not programmed by Starfleet," Data answered simply and truthfully. "My creator gave me a free will." He paused, then added, "I see now that it is more advantageous to serve you."

As Data spoke, he kept his pupils focused on the Dyrondite captain, but his optical sensors were busy examining everything he could take in by peripheral vision. He needed to locate the engineering control console, but he had no idea how to identify it amidst the crowd of alien machinery.

The captain, unaware of his guest's secret scrutiny, continued his interrogation. "We now have the means to smash your Federation. What can you offer to aid in this effort?"

Data had anticipated that question and had formulated an answer designed to target the Dyrondites' specific interests. "Aside from my enhanced physical strength, my memory banks contain a wealth of Federation records," he said, continuing to scan the bridge. "I have detailed information about technologies, cultures, star charts—"

"Weaponry and deployment?"

"Affirmative."

"Tactics?"

"Affirmative."

Gil-Pon Ldaaq considered. "What assurance do we have that you will not change loyalties again?"

Once again, Data had an answer ready. "Yours is a superior society. It would be impractical for me to remain in league with inferiors."

Just as Data finished speaking, he spotted it—a schematic of the warship on what he presumed was the engineering control console. Data's optical sensors quickly magnified the image so that he could locate main engineering, but as the shape of the schematic became clear, the android felt a jolt of surprise—it wasn't the same ship that had landed on Arunu's surface.

Gil-Pon Ldaaq's bulging eyes were studying the living machine before him. "We accept you," he announced bluntly.

Data hardly noticed that he'd successfully completed the first phase of his mission. Instead he blurted, "Excuse me, Gil-Pon Ldaaq, but am I not aboard the ship I observed landing on the surface of Arunu?"

Gil-Pon Ldaaq made a strange clicking sound deep in his throat. If the Dyrondites possessed emotions Data would have suspected that it was a form of laughter. "No, android. The vessel on the surface is a shuttle. The *Khemtk* is in orbit." Before Data knew how to react, the alien captain declared, "You are now a subject of the Ruling House. You will serve us best by giving your life to our robotics experts. Your memory core will be dumped into our systems and you will be disassembled and analyzed so that we may construct more of your kind. Confine him!"

At their captain's order, the guards raised their weapons. Data stepped back in alarm, only to bump up against a bulkhead. "Wait, this is not what I—"

His words were cut short as he suddenly dematerialized.

This time Data rematerialized in a bare room, not a brig cell but efficiently sealed nonetheless. There simply was no door.

The android stood alone, unmoving, realizing that, despite his success at deception, everything had gone wrong. He'd misinterpreted Pon Shaab's words from the start, presuming that the *Khemtk* itself would land on Arunu. He wasn't on the surface anymore, he was aboard a ship in orbit. If he sabotaged the ship, he'd never escape. If he didn't sabotage the ship, he faced disassembly by the Dyrondites. No matter what he did, his fate was sealed. "Cold hard facts, Data," came Fantico's voice from his memory banks. "Cold hard facts."

Those facts also told him that his life, though precious and unique, was nothing compared to the billions who would suffer if the Dyrondites' plans succeeded. There was only one thing to do—he would complete his mission, whatever the cost. After all, he still had the cobiem charge. If his life had to end, he would end it by stopping the Dyrondites.

Data began a swift examination of the bulkheads. They were solid, but the deck above was composed of panels that looked as if they could be opened. However, there was no way for him to reach up that far.

Kneeling down, Data opened his forearm access panel and removed the cobiem charge so that he could regain

the full use of that arm. After stuffing the charge into his pocket, he turned his attention to the metal deck plates beneath him.

No human or even Dyrondite could have lifted the plates. They were a meter square and weighed more than two hundred pounds each. But after patiently pushing his fist down near the edge of one, Data managed to dent it enough to cause the edge to buckle up. Prying his fingers underneath the tiny opening, he lifted the plate up enough to grasp it firmly, then quietly moved it aside.

Data had never seen a Dyrondite ship before, but it was practically a given that all starships contained crawl spaces between bulkheads. Such spaces offered the only way to gain access to the maze of wiring and circuitry that wove its way throughout the hull. But Data was no Dyrondite engineer. As he lowered himself into the crawl space, he realized that one wrong move, one touch of the wrong circuit or power transformer, and he could fry his own systems to a crisp.

On the other hand, if he could locate a main transformer, he could place the cobiem charge directly on it. If he was lucky, the vibrations would affect a crucial system. If he was luckier still, the results would disable the ship.

As he crawled carefully between decks, Data internally analyzed the *Khemtk*'s schematic that he'd obtained from the bridge. Main engineering was located on aft Deck Seven, but that precious information was useless now. Without knowing exactly where he was at the moment, how could he know which direction to go to get to aft Deck Seven? All he knew for certain was that the loading of the *tsidi* wouldn't take much longer. As soon as the shuttle returned, the *Khemtk* would leave orbit.

After tedious maneuvering around glowing junction boxes and blinking access panels, Data elbowed his way up to a long, bulky apparatus that looked as if it might be a Dyrondite version of a main transformer. There was no way to be sure, but he had little time to consider the matter.

Pulling the cobiem charge from his pocket, Data wedged it firmly into a groove in the unit's containment module. Then he set it for maximum pulse and activated it. Unable to calculate how long it would take the cobiem to build up a strong vibration, Data figured he might have enough time to attempt escape, however slim his chances. First he put some distance between himself and the transformer, and then he lifted up the bulkhead panel in front of him. Sliding it aside, he dropped through the ceiling onto the deck below.

"We have him!" reported a War Guard, shoving Data forward.

Gil-Pon Ldaaq gazed down at the android. "What have you done?" he demanded, his emotionless tone still conveying a sense of urgency.

Data had made the mistake of dropping down right into the middle of a security detachment. More ironic than that, the security detachment had been on its way to Data's confinement room because sensors indicated that he'd disappeared. Data had been recaptured and now stood on the bridge once again.

But the bridge wasn't a scene of humming efficiency

anymore. Lights blinked wildly, a red alarm light was flashing like a panicked heartbeat, and the officers were scrambling at their controls. "What have you done, android?" Gil-Pon Ldaaq repeated.

In truth, Data couldn't answer the question because he really wasn't sure what he'd done. For all he knew, the cobiem charge was now causing the shipboard plumbing to back up. Gil-Pon Ldaaq took a threatening step toward him just as an officer reported, "We cannot pinpoint the cause, Gil-Pon. If the disruption continues to build, we will lose control of the plasma injector."

If Data could have gasped in shock he would have. By accident he'd placed the cobiem charge on one of the worst places possible: a transformer leading directly to a major component of the warp engines. If the Dyrondites lost control of the plasma injector, the engines would overload and the ship would explode—

"One last time, android," said Gil-Pon Ldaaq urgently. "What have you done?"

Before Data could answer, the officer said, "Gil-Pon, we must evacuate. Now." At those words, all heads turned to the captain, whose face remained passive, as if nothing at all were amiss. But the force with which he grabbed Data and literally threw him across the bridge revealed the captain's opinion of the present circumstances.

"Order immediate evacuation of all decks. Use the transporters. Leave the android aboard." And with that, he entered the turbolift. After activating the shipwide evacuation signal, the other officers followed. The turbolift door closed and Data, once again, was alone.

He picked himself up from the floor where he'd

landed and analyzed his predicament. An uncontrolled flow of plasma into the warp engines would overload them very quickly. He might have two minutes, maybe three, before they exploded.

He ran to the turbolift and, with effort, pried the doors apart. The empty shaft yawned below, dark and silent. Maybe he could climb down to the deck where the transporter was located, but what deck would that be? Data didn't know. There wasn't enough time to search the whole ship. He had to find another way of escape.

Then he remembered the Dyrondite transporter tag still stuck to his uniform. Twice the device had remotely activated the shipboard transporter and locked it onto his signal. If he could figure out a way to trigger it himself, the transporter might automatically beam him to the last programmed destination—that of the evacuating crew. He had no idea where that might be, but in less than a minute, anywhere would be better than the bridge of the *Khemtk*.

He had to rip his uniform sleeve to get the thing off. Like a Starfleet commbadge, it was a round disc that opened up to reveal tiny circuitry, some of which Data recognized from the *teu qitm*. Being practical people, the Dyrondites apparently believed in using standardized components.

As the bulkheads around him began to rumble ominously, Data carefully pressed his thumbnail down on the tag's signal relay circuits, effectively shorting out the command contacts. The device activated, and just before the bridge burst into a ball of flame, he dematerialized.

CHAPTER

11

The next thing Data knew, he was back in the cavern where the cadets had first discovered the Dyrondite scientists with their stolen *tsidi.* He was also facing Gil-Pon Ldaaq, who had wrapped his strong, bony fingers around Data's throat the second Data was fully materialized. "I do not know how you escaped, android, but you will not escape this time," the Dyrondite threatened.

Data didn't move. He could easily overcome Gil-Pon Ldaaq, but not the rest of the *Khemtk* crew, all of whom stood facing him, weapons drawn, just waiting for him to give them an excuse to shoot. The *Khemtk*'s transporter must have been set to these coordinates in order to beam up the scientists ahead of the *tsidi* shipment. Instead, Data's tamperings had resulted in the crew, along with Data himself, beaming down to the cavern.

"Stop! Let go of him, now!" Fantico stepped out of hiding, wielding a rifle-type weapon that Data recognized as one of the archaeologists' sonic drill guns. Set to maximum radius, it made an effective weapon.

In response, every War Guard who had been aboard the *Khemtk* trained its weapon on Fantico.

"Drop 'em, boys." Spinaker rose up from behind a stalagmite as Professor Tesh and several other archaeologists appeared from other hiding places. All had sonic drill guns aimed and ready. "These drills are set for maximum radius," Spinaker warned. "We can wipe you out with a single combined burst. Stalemate, gentlemen."

Gil-Pon Ldaaq maintained his hold on Data, who remained perfectly still. The War Guards, taking their cue from their commander, maintained their aim on Fantico. "You would not risk Starfleet cadets," the Dyrondite captain stated flatly, "especially the android."

" 'Fraid I would," answered Spinaker. "Sorry, Data. No hard feelings?"

"No feelings at all, sir," Data replied, presuming that the professor was engaged in his own deception, though he wasn't altogether sure.

Gil-Pon Ldaaq twisted his mantis-head back and forth, evaluating the situation. "You would not risk a diplomatic situation by firing on me or my fellows. Surrender and we will not fire upon you."

"No, instead you'll just take a few *tsidi* and possibly start a galactic war." Spinaker smiled grimly. "I'm willing to risk a little diplomatic upheaval. What are *you* willing to risk?"

Slowly Gil-Pon Ldaaq released his grasp on Data's neck. The War Guards dropped their weapons. Even though they far outnumbered their foes, the Dyrondites knew that a massacre would lead to a full Starfleet investigation. Dyronda would face the Federation's wrath without even gaining one *tsidi* for its troubles. Their plan was ruined. Violence would prove impractical and most inefficient at this point.

Zhu appeared from behind Fantico, and the two cadets began gathering up the Dyrondites' weapons as the archaeologists, keeping aim with their drill guns, covered them.

"I am very *very* glad to see you, Data!" Zhu said as he tossed disruptor after disruptor into a far corner of the cavern.

"I be very *very* glad to be back," Data responded. "However, I am somewhat confused. How—"

"—did we know to be here?" Fantico grinned. "It's a long story, but first let's get these guys disarmed and secured."

Dear Diary,

I believe it is safe to say that the Dyrondite crisis is over. I consider myself most fortunate to have escaped the destruction of the *Khemtk*. The Dyrondite crew was able to escape in time as well.

I also consider myself fortunate to be part of my particular xenoethnography team. Despite the windstorm last night, Cadets Fantico and Lniuhta'bihd convinced the archaeologists to travel to the Dyrondites' secret cavern in an attempt to catch Pon Shaab by surprise. Not only did they succeed in their endeavor, but they were still present when the *Khemtk*'s ground transport arrived and later when I and the *Khemtk*'s crew made an emergency beamdown. Armed with sonic drill guns, the archaeologists captured the ground transport and were later able to surround the *Khemtk*'s crew before they fully materialized. All of the Dyrondites have been placed in the Pit. As Professor Spinaker describes it, "It's a tight fit down there," but it is the only secure holding area available.

Among Pon Shaab's supplies hidden in the cavern was the high-powered transmitter he used to communicate with the Ruling House of Dyronda. Professor Spinaker has used this unit to send a message to Starbase 25. A starship is on its way.

Sincerely,
Data

Four days later, back at Starfleet Academy, Data was called into Admiral Burkes's office. When he arrived he found Zhu, T'Pira, Lukas, and Fantico already there. T'Pira's arm had been healed by an Academy doctor, and Lukas was nearly recovered as well.

"Cadet Data," said Muti, "I thought you'd like to know that I've just received word from Arunu. Your modified *teu qitm* has been used by Spinaker's people to locate more than twenty psychic dumps on the main Arunuan continent, all with broken *tsidi* batteries inside. And Cadet T'Pira, thanks to your unintended contact with one of the batteries, Professor Spinaker was able to convince two Vulcan Kolinahr Masters to travel to Arunu and examine these sites. They were able to safely touch the battery remains, and the impressions they received allowed them to unravel the mystery of Arunu.

It seems, cadets, that the Arunuan people destroyed themselves."

Everyone but T'Pira reacted with surprise, even Data. "How, sir?" he asked.

Burkes looked grave as he explained, "The art form known as *tsidi,* which contained pleasurable emotions for entertainment purposes, eventually led to a cultural practice known as *tsidaduu.* It was a ceremony in which the Arunuans tried to cleanse themselves of all negative emotion by transferring it into large, specially designed *tsidi,* which they then buried, thinking it cleverly disposed of. But they underestimated the power of the psychic energy they'd trapped, and when an earthquake broke the *tsidi* in several of the dump sites, it caused a chain reaction that destroyed them all. The energy was released, and the Arunuans and their world were completely wiped out."

For all of his speculation about why the amazing Arunuan people had disappeared, self-destruction had never occurred to Data. He had wondered if they'd warred against each other, using *tsidi* batteries as weapons. His Federation history class had already studied several cultures that had destroyed their own planets by war. Even Earth had teetered on the brink of nuclear destruction in the 20th century. Data had also considered the possibility that the Arunuans had been invaded, and that the *tsidi* batteries had been a last-ditch attempt to stop the enemy. He'd never considered that planetwide destruction had been the result of an accident.

"Cadet Fantico," said Burkes, interrupting Data's thoughts.

"Yes, sir," Fantico responded.

"You will receive a special citation in your records for excellent leadership during the Arunu events. Cadets Data, T'Pira, Whitlock, and Lniuhta'bihd, you will receive citations for bravery. Professor Jeffrey Spinaker is quite impressed with all of you. So am I." Before the cadets became further embarrassed, Burkes dismissed them. "Oh, one more thing, Cadet Data—"

"Yes, sir?" Data said, remaining behind as the others filed out.

Admiral Burkes stood up from his chair. "Cadet, I've been given authorization to grant you access to the advanced research labs here at the Academy. Several of the professors would like your input on their projects, and you're encouraged to continue your studies of Dyrondite technology. Now that they've been identified as being a potential threat to the Federation, we need all the insight we can get. You have a surprising understanding of the Dyrondites and their technology."

Although Burkes had just given him a great compliment, the very thought of being compared to the Dyrondites created a sense of unease in Data. He attempted a casual shrug. "That may be true, sir," he said, "but I am pleased to note many differences between myself and the Dyrondites—differences that I hope will never change."

Burkes smiled and dismissed the android, who left his office to hurry after his friends.

About the Authors

BOBBI JG WEISS and DAVID CODY WEISS met and got married by mail, kind of like Sea Monkeys. At first they agreed never to send photographs to each other, so Bobbi thought David looked like Mel Gibson and David thought Bobbi looked like Flipper. It was a romance made in heaven, if you like fish.

When they finally met face-to-face, Bobbi was amazed to see that David looked about as much like Mel Gibson as the living room sofa did. Likewise, David was amazed to see that Bobbi really did look like Flipper. They could have opened a slam-dance nightclub, but they decided to become writing partners instead.

Among the books they've written are two additional *Star Trek: Starfleet Academy* novels (*Lifeline* and *Breakaway*); a *Secret World of Alex Mack* novel entitled *Close Encounters!*; two *Sabrina, the Teenage Witch* books (#1 novelization and #3 *Good Switch, Bad Switch*); and *Are You Afraid of the Dark?* novels entitled *The Tale of the Shimmering Shell, The Tale of the Ghost Cruise,* and *The Tale of the Stalking Shadow.* They recently finished writing their books *Sabrina Salem On Trial,* and *Go Fetch!*

Bobbi and David plan on writing many more books in the future, even though Bobbi has trouble typing with her fins.

**Pocket Books presents a new,
illustrated series for younger readers based on the hit
television show:**

STAR TREK
DEEP SPACE NINE®

Young Jake Sisko is looking for friends aboard the space station.

He finds Nog, a Ferengi his own age, and together they find a whole

lot of trouble!

Published by Pocket Books

954-10